PRIVATE
MEANS

Also by Cree LeFavour

Lights On, Rats Out

PRIVATE MEANS

A NOVEL

CREE LEFAVOUR

Grove Press
New York

Published simultaneously in Canada
Printed in the United States of America

First Grove Atlantic hardcover edition: May 2020
First Grove Atlantic paperback edition: August 2021

Text design by Ashley Prine
This book was set in Scala with Frutiger
by Tandem Books

ISBN 978-0-8021-4889-6
eISBN 978-0-8021-4890-2

Library of Congress Cataloging-in-Publication Data is available for this title.

Grove Press
an imprint of Grove Atlantic
154 West 14th Street
New York, NY 10011

Distributed by Publishers Group West

groveatlantic.com

21 22 23 24   10 9 8 7 6 5 4 3 2 1

For Dwight Garner

Friday, May 25,
Memorial Day Weekend

Spotting the phone charger, she unplugged it from the wall by the nightstand and threw it onto the bed where the hard, white cube clattered against the fiberglass rim of the tennis racket. Tossing orange swim trunks she found hanging inside the closet in the same general direction, Alice again scanned the space before leaving the battered leather weekend bag for Peter to stuff, zip, and carry. Entering the kitchen, she pressed her bare foot to the side of the half case of 2018 Domaines Ott Bandol and slid it across the scratched oak floorboards to the door.

She'd offered a reward. Would she be forced to demand a photo of Maebelle sitting on that day's newspaper? Would the *Post* be too tawdry? She should insist on the *Times*. The insanity of it. This wasn't Somalia or Afghanistan or the Philippines; it was Manhattan's Upper West Side—and Maebelle was a dog.

Standing at the kitchen counter, waiting for her husband to move toward the door but not daring to rush him—he was quick to snap lately—she thought of the dog's future face. Unnaturally aged, the muzzle grizzled and eyes flat, the geriatric canine profile persisted in her mind. It was nothing like the image on the LOST DOG flyer featuring Maebelle's eager, adorable mug, her nose practically touching the camera lens.

LOST DOG

$2,000 REWARD

NO QUESTIONS ASKED

Do NOT Chase

Last seen May 17th in Riverside Park

at 97th St. Please call:

914-219-8331

Microchip Number: 4689654234566

No, she would not be putting up these posters on every available surface in the neighborhood five years from now. It had been just over a week. When would she give up? In two months? A year? How long was long enough?

He'd left his office door open. Two rooms away she could discern the distinctive inflection of her husband's official doctor voice on the phone.

Yes, Wellbutrin 300 XL, and the patient does not want the generic . . . No. DAW, dispense as written.

Waiting for him to finish the call, she remembered taking her twin daughters, Bette and Emile, to a 4-H fair upstate when their chubby legs were just sturdy enough to walk in a crowd—maybe three or four years old. Biting her cuticles, the ragged skin around her nails desperate for a manicure, she recalled the heat of that dusty August day as they waited in line for funnel cakes. She'd been transfixed by a photograph of a teenager on a LOST CHILD poster. The girl's face was somehow off, but she hadn't been able to identify what was wrong with it until she read the fine print below the photograph. Her name was Kaylee, and she had been taken from that same 4-H fair. She'd disappeared at just four years old; the photo on the poster was a computer rendering of the girl at fourteen, her nose transformed from a fleshy button into a bony structure, her jawline formed into a too-perfect half oval like the sharp end of an egg, her eyes set deep in their sockets beneath well-defined eyebrows. The artist had even glossed her with lipstick—or at least it looked as if she were wearing something on her unsmiling cherry mouth. In the bottom left corner Alice had studied the then decade-old original image, circulated when the little girl had disappeared. She could have been Bette or Emile's classmate.

At the time, Alice had thought they should have done a better job with the fourteen-year-old face—made her prettier without cheapening her with makeup—if only to offer the parents the insufficient solace of holding in their minds a more pleasing image of their lost daughter. Maybe they never thought of her as a teen. Perhaps it didn't matter—she would always remain the girl they'd known for just four years, with her babyish soft, brown curls and pouty lips.

Lost in her thoughts, she turned to see Peter gathering his keys and wallet from the tray in the hallway, weekend bag in hand.

All set? she asked as cheerfully as possible.

I think so. You sure you don't want to come? It would be good for you.

I can't. I have to keep looking. As she said it, she felt her throat tighten, the grief of the loss strangling her next words. Peter mercifully broke the silence she created.

Okay. I'll see you Monday night. Love you. And with that he leaned in for a goodbye kiss.

Alice moved into it but rather than kissing him properly turned her head at the last moment, aiming her lips for his freshly shaved cheek to dodge direct, possibly wet contact with his mouth. The fruity potency of his drugstore shampoo fresh on his wet hair as they made brief contact brought back long afternoons reading fat Russian novels while sucking sour apple Jolly Ranchers.

Peter's absence, as the door's lock clicked behind him, immediately inundated Alice's senses. It was as if a draft had cooled the apartment. In its wake, the atmosphere thinned, the room's barometric pressure seeming to drop, taking Alice to a curiously open, airy space in which all that remained was her now-familiar canine grief and the promising prospect of a thoroughly chilled Chablis.

Trying to focus on the immediate physical pleasure of the crisp, cool wine filling her mouth, Alice opened the BBC app on her phone and woke her laptop. She recalled her grad school days as she tasted the minerality of the expensive wine. When they'd met, Peter had seemed old—and already a doctor. She'd been practically squatting in a decrepit studio apartment in Harlem, paying for her steady diet of yogurt, apples, peanut butter, and rice cakes on student loans and a tiny stipend from Columbia. Now she was navigating past the worries in her Google email tab to the pleasures of Posh-mark, Luxury Closet, and Thredup. Scrolling through shirts, pants, bags, and sweaters, she added items to her various shopping bags. No sale would be completed, no shipping terms selected, no boxes ticked to match billing and shipping addresses. The harmless recreational activity would not cost her a cent.

At fifty-one, she was well into the pitiless softening of her body as time conspired with gravity to ruthlessly work over every cell of skin, cartilage, and muscle. Just in the past year she'd observed the fine crepe of the skin on her thighs. It reminded her of seersucker. The dewy plumpness of her nineteen-year-old daughters' legs, arms, and cheeks came on as a surprise, their creamy beauty and ripe potential years removed from her own blighted physicality.

She'd been careless in the sun. Patches of liver-colored scale covered her arms and chest while the rest of her body was lightly doodled with odd freckles, cherry angiomas, and moles. Fifteen years of hair dye had resulted in a shade much lighter than her original brunette as the streaks of what had begun as highlights came to dominate the whole. It was no accident; her colorist had taken pity on her, incrementally lightening larger and larger swaths to cover the gray, manipulating the powerful chemicals to keep the effect as far removed as the art allowed from the brassy orange hue that crassly announced its artificiality under the fluorescent light of every New York City bathroom and subway car. For all of this, Alice was still pretty, with a wild, rangy look that matched her Northern California roots.

Running her fingers through her hair from the center part back, she cursed her lack of mental command as she rubbed her thumb and index finger together to release a stray hair.

One more down, she thought, as the fine, expensively colored strand dropped to the floor.

If the dog had been there, she would have been in her lap, staring up at her, ears forward, listening. Alice could practically feel her pushing her cool black nose against her forearm. The dog had become an extension of herself the way the twins had as infants. Since that time, with the exception of her daughters, she'd failed at intimacy; her closeness to the dog was proof of this. There was nothing safer or more certain than the animal's affection. When she wept she'd laugh at herself for whispering, *It's okay. Shhhhhh*, kissing the dog's face, ears, back, and belly as if it were the animal that needed comforting. The dog was never in a mood when she walked back in the apartment. Rather, she was consistently met by the outsize greeting of an animal losing her cool entirely as she whined and licked and wriggled in her arms. Coming home to the empty apartment was an affront.

Alice envisioned the flood of oxytocin all the kisses released, the hormone irrigating her brain, plumping her neurotransmitters with serotonin and dopamine. No wonder she experienced the loss of the dog as a physical assault. She longed to bury her face in Maebelle's fur and inhale. As she sat, she tried to elicit the experience, the faint scent of Fritos or even, more incredibly, the traces of vanilla butter cookie—a soft, rich scent surely impossible for a dog to emit, especially one that traveled at ground level through the filth of New York City.

Peter's right foot danced left-right, right-left between the brake and the accelerator. An abandoned seltzer bottle, subject to the abrupt changes in momentum, rattled over the filthy rubber mat on the passenger side, the muffled clank of glass against the metal seat adjuster passing through the car's interior as background noise, as unidentifiable as inert gas. The bottle repeated its limited range of motion with each stop-and-go of the Memorial Day–weekend migration up the edge of the island as tens of thousands of drivers and their passengers huddled in their cars at dusk, united by the tiresome effort required to escape Manhattan.

Had he forgotten something, misspoken, or embarrassed himself? Was it the cool goodbye to Alice? Or maybe just the heavy traffic? Twenty minutes passed before Peter identified the source of his uneasiness in the noise and motion of the bottle. By this point, his nerves had been so played they erupted into a fluid rage that even he recognized as entirely out of proportion to the irritant. Without releasing his seatbelt, he leaned his six-foot-three frame sideways, his long arm effortlessly retrieving the errant bottle. Ruthlessly jamming it into the cup holder, he resisted the childish urge to hurl it out the window, manfully denying himself the satisfaction of smashing it to bits on the pavement.

Focusing on the shameful expanse of faded silver paint covering the pitted metal of his 2011 Toyota Highlander, he breathed deeply, consciously mesmerizing himself with the idea of glowing red brake lights stretching for miles in his wake, a mirror image of those before him. With his well-preserved head of dark hair, shirt sleeves rolled past the elbow, khaki pants cuffed, and driving loafers, Peter tried to relax into the drive. The proletarian dignity of his well-used car against the piercing glint of the freshly acquired Lexuses, Land Rovers, and BMWs jockeying for position around him gave him a taste of self-righteous modesty. He enjoyed the aggressive game of chicken required as cars closed in on him, bumpers hugging in an effort to gain or prevent a car length's advantage.

After twenty minutes of spirited play, he knifed the nose of the big car left, breaking free of the mess exiting onto I-95/George Washington Bridge by veering onto the shoulder to avoid a Mercedes SUV blocking the far left lane. The driver had either genuinely decided to exit at the last moment or, more likely, chosen to beat the line by going around the piled-up cars by using the less congested third lane, then cutting in at the last moment.

Asshole, Peter muttered, his righteous irritation resting effortlessly next to the knowledge that he wasn't above such sleazy tricks himself. Upright in the passenger seat of the errant Mercedes, a large black Labrador retriever sat looking as patient as its breed demanded, and yet Peter thought he detected a vague disgust with the undignified tactics of its chauffeur. The sight of the dog brought Maebelle to mind.

A car—any car—could have crippled her or, for that matter, crushed the three hundred–plus bones in her body, flattening her puny twelve pounds into a ciabatta-like round. Conceivably, she was no more than a furry heap on Riverside Drive or Broadway—but then Alice would have already discovered her. With the interminable walking and looking she'd done in the past eight days how could she not have found her body? Maybe a Staten Island landfill—if that was even where garbage went these days—was her likely end? She was just small enough that the massive rotating brushes fronting the ubiquitous New York City Sanitation Department street sweepers could have trapped her body, the neat, robotic little vehicle suctioning her into its dark metal belly where her weight would compress the foul mess of plastic bags, cigarette butts, and candy wrappers into a cozy nest.

Peter wanted the dog back. He dreaded telling his daughters. He should sue the fucking dog-walking service—yes, he would. The increasing speed of his car as it hurtled down the first open stretch of the Saw Mill Parkway energized the prospect of the great sum of money he'd win in judgment against the pricks at the doggie dot-com. The thought of revenge and physical speed proved an intoxicating combination, flooding him with an expiatory pleasure he hadn't experienced in months.

The absence of Alice's mournful, fidgety presence in the passenger seat freed his mind to drift. Peter had done his best to distract her from the dog, although he hadn't been able to convince her to leave the city for the weekend. She'd chosen to stay, to search for Maebelle and attend a pet-related meeting of some sort. He hoped he'd managed to conceal his relief that she'd chosen not to come. He'd done his best to make a show of his desire for her company just as he'd made an effort to be sympathetic in the present crisis.

How bored he was of Alice's singular preoccupation. She'd been a wreck—doing nothing but search since the dog walker somehow had allowed Maebelle to slip out of her collar during a group walk and then, of all brainless things, allowed her to disappear down Riverside Drive Park amid the nepeta, drooping bleeding heart branches, and ragged, overblown irises. What kind of half-wit did that? The dog's legs were all of four inches long. How fast could she possibly get away? The only grace he could identify in the situation was that he hadn't been the one holding the other end of the leash.

Alice joked that she'd replaced the children with the dog. More like replaced their lost years of babyhood with the dog, Peter thought. Somehow she'd managed to further infantilize an inherently dependent toy of a beast. He liked the dog—even loved it, whatever that meant—but in the end it was a not overly bright mammal they'd chosen to coddle under their roof, treating it as if it were a small, precious human. Sure, his cool attachment was roughed up by Maebelle's undeniable cuteness, a cuteness that both irritated and charmed him. A Dachshund-Chihuahua mutt, she had a compelling presence, some portion of which was due to big, soft eyes outlined in black. The liquid intelligence of these slightly protruding orbs framed a black gumdrop nose on a background of trim, tan fur.

He would have liked the dog better if he could have reconciled his disdainful jealousy. As it was, he suspected his response to the dog's presence indicated some unresolved unpleasantness about himself. But damn it. The thing was continually on Alice—sleeping curled up in her bed, on her lap, trailing her around the apartment. Wildly annoyed by the constant kissing and petting, he didn't dare acknowledge the deficiency her connection to the dog signaled. In fact, he would have been concerned for her psychological state if he hadn't been quite so put off by the indignity of her puerile preoccupation.

The likelihood of finding the dog diminished every day. People stole dogs—especially exceptionally cute dogs—just as they stole money, jewelry, or whatever else they could grab. Without an owner, a dog was an object, as anonymous and

desirable as crisp hundred-dollar bills blowing down the sidewalk. If only Maebelle were ugly or vicious or not quite so
greedy for food—she'd practically inhale even a cheap treat
out of a stranger's hand. When he'd foolishly made this point
to Alice, all she could manage was an enraged, *That's bullshit!*
What a mistake—did he never learn? If only he could practice what he knew. For a psychiatrist he could be surprisingly
tactless.

On the first evening he'd helped distribute flyers. You
couldn't walk a one-mile radius around their apartment without
seeing three dozen of the things.

If someone had her, they'd have seen the posters and
decided to keep her anyway; the longer a thief kept her the
more attached they'd become and the more unforgivable and
suspicious it would be to return her. Alice must know this. She
must be despairing. He thought about turning the car around
to be with her—but didn't.

The wine finally whittling at the burr of her thoughts, Alice
read descriptions and assessed fabric content before selecting her size. Partial to leafy green and navy blue, cautious of
dressing as a lamb when she knew she was close to mutton
and yet not ready for Eileen Fisher–baggy old lady, her fifty-one
years compounded the shopping challenge her considerable
height posed. Even if she wasn't actually buying, the clothes
must potentially fit if the process were to give her any satisfaction. The virtual acquisition required less than possession but
more than pure abstraction. The clothes and shoes and bags
must be plausible purchases were she to decide to purchase

them—always a possibility. But not even wine, an empty apartment, the tiresome BBC drama of Brexit unpardonably mixed with the devastating news of another Ebola outbreak overlain with repeated clicks of not-quite-complete acquisition could keep her from thinking about the dog.

How reckless it would be to pay a ransom, even with proof of life. After all, Alice thought, what is a reward for the return of a lost dog but an offering to pay a ransom. Sure, it was an extra inducement to give back a dog someone had found and then decided to keep. What it wasn't was a way to motivate people to search for the dog. As tempted as she was by the possibility that it would speed Maebelle's return, Alice feared her engagement in the shadowy economy. Paying a reward would complicate the happy ending she hoped for, clouding the reunion with the moral responsibility for motivating future abductors.

Her very ability to offer the reward when others could not inflamed her well-developed sense of existential hypocrisy, of how claustrophobically fucked the world had become. This claustrophobic feeling, since the girls left in the fall, had driven her to fill her waking moments with work, a realm in which she could apply facts gleaned from her research to arrive at conclusions that would advance knowledge. Knowledge. That seemed to be the one remaining absolute good in her world. The rest was too messy, awful, and complicated to order or contain.

Although Peter had made it clear he thought the ransom a waste of money—although one that he believed would ultimately not be spent and therefore not a waste at all—they could afford the $2,000. (But was it enough?) Peter had been hauling in a steady stream of patients for more than twenty years now, cramming them into neat forty-five-minute blocks from 7 AM to 6 PM five days a week. At the current rate of $400 an hour, minus the office rent and malpractice insurance, the take was enough to keep them comfortably afloat. Still, they were not above the woes and sorrows of their intellectual working class as they spent all they had on their European cheese, organic Icelandic yogurt, grass-fed meat, plus mortgage, maintenance, and college tuition. They didn't even have a country house. Anywhere else they would have been flat rich; in New York City, they got by.

Alice dreamed she had her own money. What a humiliation it was not to contribute to their household income— sometimes she wished she'd never stayed home with the girls or that she'd been more aggressive in keeping up in her field. She'd been burdened by juggling their money even if she didn't make any of it—Peter refused to log in to their bank accounts just as he refused to discuss bills, savings, or budgets. Even if she could afford the Gucci black leather open-toe heels with their playful silver horse-bit buckle or the Dolce & Gabbana ankle-boot stilettos in camel eel skin she'd added to her basket, where would she wear them? She'd lost track of herself entirely in becoming a thing she'd never dreamed she'd be. As much as the girls were everything to her, it was a dubious title she'd earned: mother. Worse, she'd traded without realizing she was making a lousy bargain. She'd never even know what she'd traded for.

She could have farmed the girls out—practically everyone in New York had a nanny. But she'd chosen not to. Sure, she'd completed her dissertation, she had her PhD—the girls were still infants then—but her progress had slowed as the reality of securing a position in her field grew more remote. Over the years she'd written articles and won a few small grants, all the while circling the big prize: a grant from the Earth Institute at Columbia. Now, the lost dog a distraction, she was behind; she needed to complete the application this year, to rush herself to the market before her insights and data grew stale and irrelevant.

The urgency of it had slammed her the moment she returned from California to settle the girls at Berkeley. Doing it would require unyielding discipline. Maybe she could convince Peter to prescribe the latest antidepressant for her, something that would help her motivation and focus: Cymbalta? Levomilnacipran? Wellbutrin? Was she depressed? She wasn't sure. Wasn't everyone? Too bad Peter would never do it.

His father, Dr. Jeremy Nutting, had made the mistake of dispensing drugs to family, diagnosing every relative's ailment from the flu to broken toes to bipolar. As a GP he had claimed expertise in all fields, and when it came to his family he didn't hesitate to deploy his authority to determine the best course. No great harm had been done, but Peter swore he would never wield his authority in the family as his father had, lording prescriptions for Valium over his mother, dispensing antibiotics to the family dog. Alice would have to see her own GP if she wanted any meds, and even then she might be referred to a psychopharmacologist. To hell with it, she thought, pouring herself another glass of wine.

Closing her laptop, she stared out the window toward the Hudson, fixing her gaze on the West Side Highway where a steady stream of cars came into and disappeared from view only to be replaced by more of the same colors and shapes. The numbing flow of vehicles moved north at what she thought of as smoking speed—slow enough to light a cigarette with the window down, the smoke swirling easily around the car's interior, the burning cigarette resting in the left hand halfway out the driver's side window. Rising, Alice retrieved the hidden pack of Camel Blues from a pouch in her purse, forced open the heavy window in the living room, and lit up. Smoking quickly, she drew hard between sips of wine, extending her hand out into the humid evening breeze between drags. She had three days to air the place out before Peter returned; she needed only twenty-four hours.

It was the day after losing Maebelle when, passing a bodega on Broadway while taping up flyers, she'd popped in for a coffee. Standing at the counter, intently focused on looking for Maebelle, her eyes had been attracted by the blue, black, red, green, and silver rows of cigarette packs arrayed neatly behind the register. It was the first pack she'd bought in fifteen years. They weren't even Camel Lights now—they were Camel Blues. Whatever they were called, maintaining the virtues of her nonsmoking mommy days had no appeal. She'd forgotten how much she missed it. To hell with it, she thought, lighting another off the first.

Indulging herself in a tasty bit of magic as she smoked, she considered the idea that she'd lost Maebelle because she loved her too much—that the loss of her was cosmic retribution, punishment of a righteous force for loving the dog as one should love only the divine. Fortunately, Alice didn't believe in God. If she believed in anything it was quantum physics, which, as it turned out, was an awful lot like believing in God. If Alice needed confirmation of the bizarre and unknowable universe, she'd found it in her work. To be a biophysicist was to admit that the physical world could not be explained; the ordering principles of the universe exceeded the intellectual capacity of the human brain. It was humbling. On the most minute level the physical world defied all laws. String theory was a framework for understanding matter that contradicted physical reality. It was magic—better than any show and entirely incompatible with fixed Newtonian principles of time, space, and movement. Although he never said as much, she suspected Peter viewed her concession to universal disorder as a form of infantile magical thinking and a possible sign of depression.

If only, Alice thought, the loss of the dog were punishment for something. What a relief that would be. As it was, her disappearance was a senseless mistake. No good could come of it, no lesson learned. It was simply another void, leaving her empty and bitter. The patina of stray dog hairs stuck to her pants, blankets, coats, and sweaters, the abandoned food dish, dry water bowl, and leash hanging by the door reminded her of her dead mother's clothes. Mrs. Foster had amassed a grand wardrobe. It was all Alice's now, though she could never wear the clothes without feeling she was borrowing them without permission—an impossibility given that her mother had been dead five years. But some essence buried in the fibers of the garments kept Alice from wearing the clothes, as if the warp of time and space was animated by their use, the electrical energy of a body in contact with the fabric bringing her prickly mother back to life.

Back at her desk, she forced her eyes to focus beyond the cars to the broad, dark expanse of the river where she followed the line of a massive tanker breaking the glassy surface of the water as it passed lazily downriver. The impotent tanker, propelled by a childish-looking red tugboat emblazoned with a giant *M*, nudged the hulking mass toward the open ocean, working against the incoming pull of the evening tide. As they slid into obscurity she noticed the traffic had stopped.

Gazing at the stopped cars, her wineglass sweating by her side, a tableau of select cars were frozen in view. Alice felt a flash of Peter's pitiful frustration at being locked in. Rationally, the worst calamity of the traffic-clogging accident that had any connection to Peter was the rudeness of making their friends wait dinner. No, she told herself, I won't indulge the ridiculous. It's not my accident—not Peter's accident— quite possibly not an accident at all. If it belongs to anyone, it belongs to unlucky strangers.

Alice tried to think nice thoughts for the imagined victims ... hoping the injuries weren't too serious, nobody had died, they had excellent insurance. But the persistence of the thought that it could be Peter and worse, much worse, the sickening flash that she wanted it to be Peter, wouldn't go away. No. Not that. Alice knew the monstrous fantasy was just a crazy reverse psychology trick of the mind when you envision the worst and then think you want something terrible to happen because you think it—the mind's prohibition against the thought forcing what is feared into the foreground. How many times had she rehearsed the grisly play, imagining Peter or the girls or all three of them, dead? When they were on school buses, city streets, subways, or planes the thought flickered, back again as fast as she could think it away.

Most likely it's just a system breakdown, thought Alice. One tiny fluctuation in traffic flow—a tailgater braking abruptly, a lousy driver tapping the brakes too frequently, someone going too slowly while texting—creating, as it would, a disproportionately large effect on the whole system. The strength of one tiny variable to change the whole from within was more alchemy than science. Ah well, thought Alice. Peter's probably already past the bridge, well on his way up the Saw Mill, the slowdown in his wake.

Swallowing another great gulp of wine, Alice pushed her phone aside, as if a few more inches would help her resist the urge to call him. Entering rooms having forgotten why she was there, locking herself out, going out for the day without her phone—these actions resulted from the relentless narrative of what she was thinking frequently getting in the way of what she was doing—or was supposed to be doing. Except when she was working. When focused on the internal dynamics of a murmuration she could deliberately bring thought and action together.

The complexities of the liquid movement of massive flocks of starlings as they collectively contracted, expanded, and twisted in eerily grandiose order never failed to hold her attention. Alice applied mathematical formulas and computer models in an attempt to explain how the birds coordinated their movements with such astonishing precision. The rapidity of communication between the masses of birds perplexed science. It was a mystery not yet unraveled in spite of the supercomputers that could crunch set upon set of numbers in three dimensions. Alice's work explained the surprising phenomenon using precise mathematical equations while still leaving a great deal to poetry. Her love of data acted as a countermeasure to the disorder of her messy room, moth-bitten sweater, unwashed hair, slightly redolent armpits, and filthy feet. Maybe that was why the fine balance between chaos and order attracted her as much as it explained her boredom with maintaining the physical details of her environment.

Grabbing a bag of apricots from the counter, she ran a tub and slid in. There was something inexplicably bewitching about eating a dozen apricots while soaking in a tub of cool water. Her sweat leaked into the chilly black water of the unlit bathroom to mingle with the porcelain along with the pits she carelessly dropped like pebbles between her spread legs. She ate the fruit greedily, biting into them one after the other. Some, soft and sweet with juice, made a mess of her chin. Others, tart and hard, came away in chunks, crisp like apples. She was feeling a little crazy but inclined to be more so. She wanted to stay in the bath forever, eating apricots until the tub filled, not with water but with hard little dark-brown stones, rough edged, bits of soft orange fruit clinging to the crevices. As it was, there were just enough to pool together in the bottom of the tub, schooling like fish seeking safety in numbers. Yes, thought Alice, stay forever.

But eventually she grew cold and practical. Slowly fishing the pits out, feeling for each one with her fingertips, she secreted them back in the damp, empty paper bag. Running the warm water, she scrubbed, the shampoo foaming on her scalp gradually displacing the grime of three days' sweat—New York City sweat—complicated by hot air forced down subway tunnels onto platforms, by sidewalks crowded with tourists who didn't know how to walk, and by wave upon wave of longing and regret.

Friday, May 25,
Memorial Day Weekend

He tried not to compare the woman he'd fallen for all those years ago—outdoorsy smell, bad-girl black jeans, highbred WASP confidence, quirky, geeky mind—to the woman he now knew. When they'd met, the seven-year age difference in his favor conferred a romantic seniority with what he hoped was a daddy-tinged sexiness of the older man heating her brain. The boon of a younger woman found its locus for him in what he'd quickly discovered was an unmarred body at the peak of physical perfection: sizable breasts high and taut, dimple-free ass that always seemed to hang halfway out of her too-small white cotton underwear, and the glorious, clean, fragrant cunt. He was evolved enough to know he must use the word only in his mind, and he did so with the greatest affection. To him, *cunt* captured a schoolboy's fear, ignorance, and lust for the forbidden object. When he went down on her he did not want to think of the urethra, labia majora, labia minora, Bartholin's glands, vulva, vagina, clitoris, and anus. But *cunt*, yes, that was a word.

The reckoning of her beauty, even now, was not insignificant. Of course he would not have married a beautiful but stupid woman. He wouldn't have even married a beautiful but uninteresting woman. Alice was complete—a brainy biophysicist out of his league—at least he'd thought so at the time. They'd had just three years of what had felt like an inevitable coupling. *It is written,* he'd whisper to himself in jest when stray moments of doubt fogged his optimism. She moved into his apartment on Bleecker Street, they mingled their debts and assets, introduced each other to their respective parents, and, within a year, were engaged and then quickly married.

Alice got pregnant too fast. What a tired cliché that was. Or should he say he got Alice pregnant too fast? It hardly mattered. A mistake? She was a scientist for fuck's sake—and he a doctor. He'd been hoping for years of blissful coupling, time for him to further establish his practice and time for her, most of all, to finish her research on the internal dynamics of starling flocks. He'd hoped she'd land a plum university or think tank job, but there hadn't been time.

When Alice, her face puffy from crying, told him she was carrying not one but two fetuses, he'd heartlessly gone out without her and gotten flat drunk on gin. Later, they talked about it but agreed an abortion wasn't for them even though Alice had already had one in college. The pregnancy of their shared future babies had felt different. As a couple they were fearful that in course, when their living children arrived, they'd be shadowed by the twins' ghosts endlessly hinting at the possibility of unknowable lost charm, intelligence, and talent. They feared the absence might cast doubt as much on their ruthless decision as on the children they chose to keep.

The twins were the end of the financial trajectory he'd vaguely wanted for himself. Whatever it involved, its focus was on nicer things—a bigger apartment with a view and no street noise, tasteful furniture he chose rather than found or inherited, luxe hotels and restaurants, and not ordering the second-cheapest bottle of wine on the list. Through his practice his father had made a good life for himself and his two children. That's all Peter wanted. Security. Sometimes he felt he'd attained it, but somehow the concept had morphed.

Alice wanted things he didn't understand. Sure, there were nicer things to have now than there were in the 1960s and '70s. Back then there had been a standard of quality that, once attained, need not be exceeded. There was such a thing as enough. Now there were seemingly unending tiers of quality, each claiming greater integrity and intrinsic value than the next. Did Alice need the $400 (at 50% off) organic duvet cover made from heirloom cotton in eco-friendly Italian mills she'd recently purchased for Bette's (now her) bed? Eight hundred dollars for a twin duvet cover? It seemed impossibly expensive, but he was humble enough to acknowledge the possibility that he simply lacked the sensibility to appreciate fine things.

Just the night before, Alice had gone on about the repulsive juiciness of a pinot noir, its lack of finish and dimension. Tossing the wine down the sink, she'd been just about to pour the remainder in the bottle down after it when he stopped her. It tasted just fine to him. He drank it happily. Alice could and would buy something better and more expensive. It never occurred to him to object. He provided for his family. It was such an old-fashioned way to think of the purpose of his work, but it was accurate. He worked to supply his family

with housing, food, wine, education, clothes, and, yes, even a
$400 duvet cover and a $36 bottle of pinot.

The years following the birth of the girls surprised him
as their tiny presences erased their identity as a couple. From
the day of their birth, Emile and Bette created a massive void
of need that they—but mostly Alice—instinctively filled with
all the time and energy they could spare without destroying
their own selves entirely. The shock that the two of them no
longer existed as an essential entity wasn't nearly as terrible as
how little that loss mattered next to the magnetic force of the
two live humans they'd made. The babies became the center
of any room they occupied, commandeering the conversation
before emitting a gurgle. What a marvel of human evolution-
ary design that even ugly babies were impossible to ignore.

On hiatus from her research and writing, the biological
inevitability of nursing her young further transformed Alice
from a cerebral creature into the most physical of beings. The
tedious procedures of pregnancy, breastfeeding, and nurturing
two small children exacted a material cost. Peter, an intimate
witness, tenderly perceived devastating loss as the girls needs
whittled away at the fiber of the woman he remembered.

The extended office hours of his busy practice freed him
to experience the life of his family as an all-female domestic
performance with guest appearances from him in the evening
and on weekends. For the first five years he was cast as the
fool—he'd arrive home in the evening to gently chase the girls,
his monster antics calibrated to provoke that uncanny fleeting
fear that elicits a child's screeching delight while stopping short
of terror and tears. He'd then bathe his little *putti*, as he liked to
call them, in towering masses of bubbles, their sexless bodies

slippery in the warm water. Snuggling them into the bed they insisted on sharing, he'd give dramatic readings of the same books again and again.

In the years of their girlhood—when they still wanted as much of him as they could have—he played the easy hero by taking them to movies, plays, the ballet, and concerts. What began with Pixar and Disney films, *Alice in Wonderland* and *Peter Pan* onstage, *The Nutcracker* and *Cinderella* in toe shoes and tutus, evolved into standard grown-up fare by the time they were teenagers. By then he had a firm bond with them around all this fancy culture—shared tastes, memories, regrets, events to anticipate. When the girls became adults in miniature, forcing their independence by closing their bedroom doors, he'd taken the parenting lead by offering himself as a more reasonable, steadier alternative to Alice. Plus—he had the ritual of all that shared culture topped off with drinks and dinner.

When the syrupy Shirley Temples had been replaced by bracing gin and tonics before the performances and buttered pasta and chicken breast after the show had become ambitious meals of dumplings and organ meats, the bit part had vanquished the lead. It was cheap on Peter's part to swoop in as the authority when Alice had thanklessly done the hard work for more than a decade—and still did much of it—but she left him no choice. By then she had frayed, the edges of her personality and sense of purpose having dissolved or moved inward after more than a decade of neglect. Peter was steadier, with a greater lust for life and a more purposeful, rewarding profession.

Peter refused to face the incongruity between the energetic potency of his love for the girls and his subdued affection for Alice. It was an uneasy truth made mentally palatable by the enduring value of loyalty and gratitude. Years of married coexistence had been cruel. His regard for her, the place she occupied in his thoughts, had been dulled by his belief that he thoroughly knew her. Peter could no longer see his wife clearly any more than he could see himself. He'd given up trying. Bored with Alice, bored with himself, it was only the girls that elicited a fierce longing in him.

The twins' departure for college nine months prior had left him isolated with Alice, and now that they'd landed prestigious internships in Berkeley, they wouldn't even be home for the summer. The winter months had been lifeless; he felt as though he were trying to breathe underwater in a toxic, oxygen-starved dead zone. Their best friends, the Donnes and the Darlings, were busy the way people were always busy these days. He and Alice attempted to make a routine of dates—movies, Chinatown, Jackson Heights for Indian food—but they struggled to sustain a conversation for more than fifteen minutes. He periodically swore to himself he'd stop looking at his phone when she was speaking, but there was vitality and excitement in the warm little device. His phone assured him he was alive. The virtual social connections he involved himself in, those communicated through photographs and one-liners, news and opinion, contained the real materiality of his and others' lives. He needed this rich substrate to sustain him beyond Alice's remote musings about work, what she was reading, or, for the past week, Maebelle.

To avoid conflict they'd become brittle and overly polite. It was a blow when Alice set up an office-bedroom in Bette's vacated room. The separate beds were the inescapable physical evidence of the state of their crippled marriage. They joked about the Lucy and Ricky arrangement, but he felt a hypocrite. How could he maintain a viable position in relation to patients struggling with their own marriages and long-term relationships? The truth of the situation humiliated him.

Peter hesitated to admit the sensual pleasures of gaining solo command of the sixty-inch-wide queen mattress. The freedom reminded him of being in his first apartment when, like all doctors in residence, he'd endured an erratic schedule. The bed in that studio apartment, the same one on Bleecker Street he later shared with Alice for three short years, had served as a haven from the brutality of his psychiatric residency at Bellevue Hospital. The quality of his sleep on that bed, pre-Alice, had been close to a sacred coma of oblivion. Twenty-three years later his solo bed in their shared apartment was once again his escape.

Too bad his sleep was so disturbed that all he had left of the sort of rest he'd experienced in those days was nostalgia. Each night, after expending the oblivion gifted to him by the booze he'd consumed, he'd wake at the pointless hour of 2 AM. After failing to return to oblivion, he'd concede to the inevitable, first opening Twitter and then the *New York Times*, *Slate*, Instagram, and finally long-form political pieces in the *New Yorker* when things got very bad. His brain alive with outrage at the messy world, he'd eventually turn off the phone and try again for sleep. But he couldn't lock himself in alone with his spiraling worries behind eyes forced closed for long. Without fully admitting it to himself, he feared he'd begun to doubt the utility of talk therapy; the imperfect bed was his best refuge from what he suspected was a looming moral failure at the core of his existence.

Google Maps had him arriving at 8:03 PM. Settling into another two hours in the car, Peter recalled his last session of the day. It had not gone well. Ben, a currency trader with what most psychiatrists would have diagnosed as intermittent explosive disorder (IED), had appeared in his office for the first time three months prior. He was there at his wife's insistence—a common but still less-than-ideal premise for treatment. Ben's resistance, already a formidable challenge in any course of therapy, was blended with explicit resentment directed at his wife and Peter as the instruments of his punishment.

What Peter couldn't quite sort out—and he should have been able to without any trouble—was how to circumvent the man's defenses. His directive as a therapist was to enter into the patient's psychic reality and then move gently along the route to positive change—allowing them, always, the lead. It should have been straightforward: outbursts of anger were frequently maladaptive reactions to fear and stress.

Ben had begun his session that afternoon with a complaint.

I can't believe I'm pissing away my time here. Again. The market's on a bender today. My position's totally gummed up. Business as usual.

Is something particularly bothering you about being here today? Peter replied. You've chosen to come—in fact, you've chosen to be on time for every one of our sessions.

Don't do late. Never have. You know, I'm just one of those people who's never late. Why are people late? Tabitha. She's late. Always fussing over something. I'll be damned if I let her make me late. I go right on ahead without. That gets her out the door.

What would happen if you were late—say, for an appointment here?

Hell if I know. Waste of money. How is that relevant? I just said I'm never late. Never.

You just said you feel you're losing money by coming here. So perhaps in the larger calculus you'd be better off coming late. But you don't. Peter wasn't at all certain where he was going with this, but there it was. It was always safe to keep a session in the present.

Damn straight I'm losing money. Every minute. And I don't mean your damn fee. That's nothing. Like I said, the market's junked up. Christ. And where am I? Here. Talking to a shrink. Now that's funny. Meanwhile, my assistant's handling thirty peak accounts. Asia's fucking off the rails today, and my positions there are more vulnerable than I'd like. You know what I mean?

Peter ignored the question as well as the insult regarding the insignificance of his fee. The closest he'd come to concerning himself with the value of the yen over the South Korean won over the Malaysian ringgit was for a fourth-grade social studies project. The best part of it had been drawing and coloring in the flags with his Lyra Aquarelle set.

Have you recently discussed how you feel about coming here with Tabitha?

She won't. I've told you that. It's either this or divorce court, and I'll be damned if I'll have my book split in two. Fuck-you money. Gives that expression a new meaning. Whatever the number is, that's the only way I'm out. What I'd give for a proper prenup right about now. What I was thinking I have no idea.

You've said you want to stay married, and in fact you've said you love Tabitha. There are other reasons to stay with her.

Fine. So?

Can you come up with other reasons for staying in your marriage? Set the money aside for a moment.

The guy was the opposite of most of the unhappily married patients he saw. They bemoaned their sexless, emotionally empty, anxiety-inducing relationships but were too delicate to admit that the real reason they wanted to avoid divorce was to protect their assets. It was funny how people lied to themselves. He supposed the mercenary impulse had its limits—even in New York.

Ben, on the other hand, was terrified his wife would leave him, but he could never admit he wanted her to stay for anything other than financial reasons. As far as Peter could see, the two had developed a comfortably familiar pattern of mutual complaint; it was what passed for a relationship in many marriages that outlasted a decade. If the routine trades across foreign currencies sustained Ben with a comforting familiarity as much as his relationship with his wife did, Bitcoin was his sexy fantasy mistress and just as unattainable. So Ben fumed as the value of the highly volatile cryptocurrency flashed on computer screens across the globe with the unpredictability of a much-too-pretty, pouty twentysomething.

Ben had jeopardized his easy marital arrangement by screaming at his wife too often about the state of the summer house or the market or the traffic or the noise coming from the apartment above. But Peter suspected the real trouble was that he'd jeopardized his financial future by playing the cryptocurrency game when nobody quite knew how. The idea of financial ruin stimulated Peter's interest in a man whom he instinctively disliked.

Okay, said Ben.

Then the air was empty. *Okay* was not a reason to stay in the marriage—it wasn't an answer at all—but Peter had grown tired of the standard shrink lines: *Can you say a bit more about that? Can you expand on that a bit? Any further thoughts?* Instead, he'd changed tack.

We talked last week about what you might be avoiding and gaining by exploding in anger at Tabitha. We discussed how you may be directing your frustration at her over your inability to control volatility in the currency markets.

—I'm avoiding her. Did I mention what a bitch she's been lately? Now what? You tell me, doc. Fix me up and send me on my merry fucking way. I have a lot on my mind. Whatever you might be thinking over there in your cushy chair, the market's still open in Hong Kong.

Peter wasn't sure what to say. Ben was quite possibly incapable of the empathy necessary to perceive his own behavior from anyone else's perspective. Ungenerously, Peter wished he'd never walked in the door. But he had. *Go to the fundamentals*, Peter told himself. What was happening between them in the room was a typically male impasse, which told Peter a great deal about how Ben operated in the world. The tension and opposition they were experiencing during their sessions was likely repeated with variation in most of Ben's relationships. Ben was trying to push Peter around, intimidating him, challenging him to take his side against his wife. It was an antediluvian form of male bonding Peter particularly disliked.

Ben feared losing his wife, his job (he'd been warned twice for violent outbursts at work), and his money (he took huge risks with each one of his trades, he was playing with Bitcoin, and his wife would probably do a number on his bank account if they were to divorce). But his inability to enter into these legitimate fears, to articulate them as human problems that affected him just as they did, in various forms, everyone else, made the fears unreal. Denied their existence in his mental landscape, they took on fantastic proportion in his subconscious mind. By refusing to admit that his somewhat ordinary fears were real, by pretending nothing was bothering him and the problem was everyone else, Ben allowed himself to remain in an artificially safe, icy space walled off from any genuine emotional response—until the outburst. His distorted perception of his wife as his persecutor fueled his desperation. Nobody behaved all that well when they were just hanging on, isolated and defending an untenable position.

After years of practice, this simple case of what was really just anger management should not have merited another thought beyond the hour. But it did. Peter prided himself on his professionalism, his steady publishing record in the *Psychoanalytic Review*, and his full roster of patients. As the Saw Mill became the Taconic, Peter entered the oppressive tunnel of greenery that made the drive north on any one of Moses's parkways numbingly monotonous. With nothing to distract him but the explosive chlorophyll of the freshly leafed-out trees, he mulled over how to bring Ben out of his resistance. The guy wasn't a sociopath even if he behaved like one. It was time for Peter to humanely state his own frustration with how the sessions were going and use that to break down the resistance Ben had been mounting since his first session. He must try to muster his compassion; it was not a thing he usually had trouble with.

Trying not to think about work, Peter focused on his weekend ahead with the Donnes. The pool, only recently filled for the season, would be unbearably cold. But he would swim. It was a point of pride to enter cold water. He and Alice always made the girls join them for the first swim of the season just as they insisted on entering Maine's icy waters in August. Avoiding cold water indicated character weakness. Submitting to the anticipated discomfort and then discovering its pleasures was a life lesson worth reinforcing.

William and Wendy Donne's Revolutionary-era house in Chatham, New York, had been restored with a preservationist's sensitivity to historic detail. The house's understated atmosphere had been achieved with the lavish application of cash. Wendy was a psychiatrist—they'd completed their residencies at NYU/Bellevue together, bonding over the rigors of managing the city's indigent insane. Unlike Alice, who seemed to have withered, Wendy had grown stout over the years. The lustiness suggested by her curvy body appealed to Peter as an expression of her acceptance of pleasure: not just food and wine but theater, concerts, books, travel, and, not least, sex. She and William had what struck Peter as a very healthy sexual relationship, with afternoon romps referred to as *naps* on the weekends on top of a set biweekly routine. The thought of it made Peter at once envious and fatigued. Wendy was loud—her opinions and laughter dominant in the rowdiest groups—while William was subdued, with the entitled air of the very rich that Peter tolerated only for Wendy's sake.

The two had married ten days after he'd married Alice; they'd had to curtail their honeymoon in Martinique to be back in time for the three-hundred-guest affair at William's parents' estate in Great Barrington. Like his father, William was at Goldman. He didn't make money for doing his job—his job was to make money. It had never crossed Peter's mind to go into a field with the singular purpose of moneymaking. But why not? Considering the steady, healthy fees he collected, he wondered what it would be like to have so much more. But he couldn't allow himself to enter a realm that separated him so starkly from his community-minded upbringing. It would feel like a betrayal of his parents, of his desire to help others, and of what he thought he still believed were his more modest values. Still. It just felt shabby not being filthy rich these days when there had once been such nobility in it.

Peter's long hours in his ergonomic analyst's chair had added weight to his frame over the winter; the belly was a distinctive feature of his silhouette. The Donnes were as deliberate about the wine they served as they were inattentive about the food they cooked. It hardly mattered. After a few drinks he would find something or other to eat too much of. He ate like a bear when drunk—as if seeking ballast for the passage through winter's night. Like most men his age, he gauged his weight by his belt, turning the objective measure of his waist into a mental game that determined his physical worth. Just that morning he'd been forced to settle into a new hole— giving his belt more length—four out from his goal, which had become more of a long-lost ideal. As he drove, he straightened his back to prevent the second fold of belly fat from pressing against the first. He liked to think he could cut back easily enough—after the long weekend. It was summer, after all. Bathing suit season.

The tires hummed obtrusively as he passed over the Croton Reservoir, the red metal scaffolding overhead giving an unfinished, inelegant industrial appearance to the bridge against the lush woods. New York City's famous raw water. Here it was, right out in the open. The idea that the water for New York City was in an open pool in the woods struck Peter as ridiculous—but then, where would it be if it weren't here? The reservoir began supplying New York City with water when it was dammed and connected to New York's first aqueduct in 1842. The tunnel and its tributaries snaked their way beneath the streets of Manhattan, crowded by basements, subway tunnels, foundations, and ancient graves. What a world: a whole metropolis of matter flowing unseen beneath the city, a design with intention.

Rounding what he affectionately recognized as the final curve, Peter soon caught sight of the Donnes' pretty white clapboard perched on the hill across from a pasture where aged horses and young Hereford steer mingled, grazing. Peter looked forward to the distant lowing of the cattle filtered through the eager racket of birds that, unless it was raining, would wake him at dawn. It was a gift to lay there in the supple bed on linen sheets, the window ajar to the outdoor world, listening to the birds carry on as the light asserted itself. He would doze in this luxurious dawn, as he had for years of biannual visits to the house, until called below by somebody scrambling a mess of eggs, their sulfur-tinged buttery richness passing through the ancient beams to his room high above.

As Peter pulled into the shared driveway of the Donne family compound, the cars parked tight at a snug diagonal, he winced at the prospect of his entrance. He could never quite spit out the names of the various friends and neighbors who lurked around the weekend's edges, their comings and goings from

meals and cocktails unnerving, the group briefly distracted as
it recalibrated to accommodate their familiar—but nonetheless
unexpected—presences.

Gathering his overnight bag but leaving his tennis racket
in the trunk, Peter hoisted the neat half-case of wine up on
his shoulder and turned toward the warm glow beaming
through the screen door. He anticipated them all gathered
there in the kitchen, waiting for him. Arriving later than he'd
planned turned his entrance into an event and, inevitably,
a performance.

They were well into their drinks, a fact most clearly
announced by the state of the once carefully composed display of local cheeses, crackers, and Italian olives that had been
reduced to an unappetizing scattering of crumbs, masticated
olive pits, and waxy cheese rinds. Thanks to his tardiness, the
drinking had continued without movement toward the dinner table. The mess of the cheese board would be there until
morning, giving the unlucky first to rise a further shock in
their state of bleary dehydration as they entered the dispiriting
disorder of the kitchen.

In bed, acutely missing the presence of the dog tucked under
the covers to her left, Alice listened sleepily to Peter's postmor-
tem snark. He whispered into the phone from what he called
the two W's guest room in the country, his library voice made
sloppy and silly by drink. He studiously avoided any mention
of the dog.

Of course they made pasta, Peter whispered to Alice from
the dark of his bed. I told you they would. A giant pile of

bucatini with nothing beyond a few pine nuts and basil to make it worth eating. I added an obscene pile of Parmesan. I think Wendy thought I was drunk, a giant airy mound of shavings—it was like an anthill of cheese. To hell with a polite dusting. Fuck it. Would it kill them to cook a little protein?

Goodnight, P., she said. Talk tomorrow. Love you.

Alice hadn't had a decent orgasm in six months. Masturbating with a pet in the bed felt awkward and a shade off, but Maebelle had grown used to the noise and movement and generally slept through the whole proceeding. Now she was gone.

Prone beneath the weightless duvet, warm and clean after her bath, Alice considered retrieving her toy. She might lull herself to sleep but hesitated at the prospect of a mediocre orgasm. Tucked snugly inside a white felt shoe bag on the shelf next to her bed, it was certainly handy. Two years ago she'd bought the slim appliance on Amazon. With its smooth, ballerina-pink silicone exterior and rounded ergonomic handle, it looked and sounded like the Clarisonic buffer she maneuvered over the contours of her face each night before bed.

Peter, spotting the buffer in the bathroom, couldn't resist saying, Oh, so that's what you're up to in there. Alice had rebuffed him, scoffing at his feigned ignorance.

Oh please, she'd said with a laugh. Imagine away, bristles and all.

The real, distinctly bristle-free item was fantastic, no question. But for some reason it had been delivering less-than-overwhelming results lately. The always-waiting porn on her phone rested not even a foot away from her head, the screen still glowing from Peter's call.

Alice thought back to her first Mac computer, a clunky oversize machine in garish pink that had filled the depth of her broad desk. It had seemed sleek and elegant—back when it was. Then, the cozy bed-bound laptops, phones, and iPads, as easily slipped between the sheets as tucked in a bra, didn't exist even in Steve Jobs's expansive imagination. Now the slick devices had taken over, occupying every moment as forcefully as a species of highly demanding house pet.

To soften the edge of her feminist guilt, Alice liked to think her incorporation of the seedy terrain of fleshy images into her mental and physical landscape was fairly innocent. Tentative and incremental, she'd started with Gustav Klimt's *Woman Seated with Thighs Apart*, one of the images that populated the margins of the masturbation Wikipedia entry. Another of Alice's favorites in those early days was Peter Johann Nepomuk Geiger's 1840 watercolor depicting a monk in drab robes fingering a woman, the folds of her green skirt, white stockings, and full thighs rendered in exquisite detail as her left hand grips the erect penis visible at the parting of his robe. Alice was vaguely troubled by the forceful valence of the painting. In her mind, the monk had pursued the woman whose willing acquiescence made the stealthy act so steamy.

Whatever she discovered, googling the word with the purpose of getting off on the text and images lined up to define it had been subversive enough to get her blood moving. It all seemed quaint now. When the utility of the sexually relevant Wikipedia entries had been spent (cunnilingus, sex, pornography), she progressed to erotica. There, selecting the category constituted the most terrifying confession of desire: lesbian, incest, voyeur, bondage, S&M. Forced to make up her mind,

Alice confronted her erotic triggers as an array of choices as long as a folio-size laminated diner menu. Deciding on one put her in direct contact with her subconscious; she'd had no idea what excited her until it was revealed by her physical response to the categories. She was more subversive than she'd ever admitted to herself, her taste for public sex and lesbian scenes entirely at odds with her history.

She'd arrived at the porn gala late and, she liked to think, reluctantly, wearing no makeup and a frowsy flannel night-gown. But she had arrived. Now, reaching for her phone and felt bag, she was reminded for the second time that day of her childhood and of hours of naughty pleasure passed eating sweets under the covers with a flashlight and a novel.

Sunday, May 27,
Memorial Day Weekend

It was less cocktail party than wake. Six strangers in private mourning. But Alice wanted her dog—they all did—so she remained positioned around the vast round glass coffee table, her lanky body perched tensely on the edge of one of two semi-circular white leather sofas. Ten exquisitely groomed toenails lay displayed through the glass, magnified as if seen through clear water. Red. Navy. Frosted Pink. Fuchsia. Her own dark camouflage, nearly identical to the rich green coccolithophore, a phytoplankton that had been the subject of her first serious research project in high school. An adjacent pair of amber leather loafers complimented her green.

All but one of the group were slugging back a resinous cabernet sauvignon the color of dried blood. A leathery woman who somewhere along the way had decided overprocessed white-blonde hair, red lipstick, and heavy mascara was the look she wanted, took frequent sips of her conspicuously clear beverage, the fetal lime wedge resting on an ice shelf within a testament to what she suspected was nothing so fun as gin but rather an inefficient gesture to accommodate sobriety in a room of drinkers.

Five desperate women and a token male, each one missing a dog, brought together by a string of Facebook posts on Manhattan-Lost-Dog. After a flurry of public posts, a group had peeled off into a private discussion with the private discussion leading to a gathering on a Memorial Day weekend Sunday evening. The decision to meet in person felt old-fashioned and dangerous. The easily dismissed text on Alice's screen was embodied before her—each with a face, voice, mannerisms, style, and scent of his or her own.

How had she ended up here, in this impossibly wealthy woman's apartment, high above the twinkling lights that formed the perimeter of the unlit lagoon of Central Park? Could she ever be friends—or even friendly—with any of them? It seemed unlikely, though she eyed the sole male member of the group, assessing the French cuffs of his Charvet shirt. She felt herself as separate from them all as the neatly white-aproned maid surely felt from the guests she served, discreetly passing the smoked salmon canapés, moving among them as invisibly as possible—eyes down, frequent nods, a flash of a smile and understated nod in place of *You're welcome*. Who kept a maid in uniform anymore, anyway? The ensemble, from the white piping on the black shirtdress to the scalloped edge of the linen apron to the lace headpiece, suggested a bawdy bedroom farce. Alice tried not to catch anyone's conspiratorial eye; she was afraid she'd start laughing. Fortunately—or not—there were none to be found.

Jody, sitting next to the hostess directly across the table from Alice, was telling the story of losing her dog in Central

Park two months ago. Alice suddenly had a feeling for how many people she must have bored with her own story.

I let her off leash like always near Sheep Meadow. She loves to run. She's so good. I mean, she never bothers anyone. And then—

Alice tried to pity her but all she could do was assess the Pucci purse, Thierry Rabotin wedges, asymmetrical Botox effect around the eyes, and jeans that a woman hovering around sixty should long since have handed down to her daughter—or granddaughter. Jody's dog Pug was not a pug. He was a French bulldog. An expensive one. Everything about this woman was expensive. Alice did not feel sorry for her until she reminded herself that Jody had also lost her dog. She was there for the same reason Alice was—in hopes that someone would offer a fresh strategy to find her dog. But Alice, peering sideways at Jody's fetching suede navy wedges, could only think, *Pay somebody to find your dog.* Of course, she noted, that was perilously close to what she was doing with her paltry $2,000.

The chatter of the women's stories featuring themselves and their exceptional dogs was muted by the baby talk that crept in from the edges. The dogs' names were invariably babyish, even without the high-pitched and singsong lilt that seeped into the women's voices. Never mind the dogs weren't there to perk up their ears. Alice was as guilty as the rest of them. Maebelle: a proper name for a glitter-sprinkled fairy in a Disney film or, at best, for a chubby, rosy-cheeked five-year-old with silky blonde ringlets. What had she been thinking?

Okay, let's get started, Julie said above the din, straightening her Pilates-tuned back to its full length, putting her formidable breasts on glorious display. She, the venerable hostess of the cabernet, had lost her dog Sebastian ten days ago. The reward offered for returning the golden-haired Tibetan mastiff was a cool $10,000. Alice absently wondered if she'd be given the award if she came across Sebastian. She supposed that would be crass. She'd have to at least pretend not to want it. *I couldn't*, she heard herself saying without conviction, as she led the fluffy beast past liveried doormen in the vast, marbled lobby.

Ladies! And gent, Julie said with an affected giggle worthy of Lucy Steele. Alice stared at her, unsmiling, torn between pity and the tiniest glint of embarrassment.

I've printed out resources.

She handed a stack of flyers to Jody on her left. Alice took one, passing the last one to Nancy. She'd done her homework— or someone had done it for her.

- ☐ FindShadow.com
- ☐ HelpingLostPets.com
- ☐ LostMyDoggie.com
- ☐ PawBoost.com
- ☐ PetAmberAlert.com
- ☐ Petfinder.com
- ☐ LostDogsofAmerica.org
- ☐ FidoFinder.com
- ☐ craigslist.com
- ☐ Bestfriends.org

At the bottom of the page she'd listed several Facebook groups alongside two private investigators.

I know most of you are familiar with these but I thought it would be useful to be sure each and every one of you checked off all the boxes.

She'd actually printed empty squares to mark next to each source.

Now, there's International Counterintelligence Services, what I call ICS, which is the only way to go if there's any chance your dog has been taken overseas. Trust me. But the real star and just a bun of a woman is a Karen Tarnot and her incredible team of sniffer dogs out of Iowa—or is it Idaho? It doesn't matter. I simply can't say enough about Karen.

She then paused, appearing to need a moment to stifle a tear before continuing.

Don't even consider using an unlicensed pet detective. Karen's just magnificent and would have found Sebastian but the urban environment is so, so difficult—

Alice tried to overlook her sorry performance of a crisp BBC accent. Perhaps the affectation hid shamefully soft, long vowels and dropped consonants originating in obscure Southern roots her husband's millions had effaced. The fuchsia toe polish, hulking diamond solitaire, and French tips said *Yes*.

Amid the rustle of papers and low chatter, Alice considered the gathering from above, her disembodied self in a scene it was almost unsporting to despise; the elevator doors had opened on the set of an overproduced Netflix series bent on pillorying New York's monied elite.

The Christopher Wool and Rudolf Stingel pieces Alice sat staring at as Julie droned on about the advantages of a private detective were just set pieces, but they pulled her in, their astonishing presence in the intimacy of the living room deeply incongruous. She'd never seen a Wool or a Stingel outside of a gallery.

When her mother had died, she'd sold the art—*my collection*, as her mother had preposterously put it. Alice and Peter had counted on at least a quarter-million dollars from the sale of the forty-some paintings and prints. They had planned to pay off college loans and stash the rest. But then, *The market's just not what it was ten years ago, tastes change*, intoned Lawrence, the head of fine art, Bonhams Los Angeles. There wasn't a single piece worth his time.

To have what seemed like tangible ready money evaporate into nothing felt like a loss. Expectation did that. Oh well. Alice had kept a few of the pieces she'd stared fondly at as a girl, but the gloss had diminished, as if the absence of commercial value had eroded their allure.

Falling into the center of the Wool, Alice released all thoughts of the painting's worth. She simply wanted the screen print in her bedroom to stare at, to commune with, to study and know until it became hers. She wanted to master its inexplicable potency. There was nothing extraordinary about the fairly plain, inky black blob—except that there was. Similar to a Rorschach inkblot, it evoked psychological complexity with its undefinable shape tapping into iconic sexual motifs. Was she drawn to it as a relic containing a trace of the artist's essence? She didn't care: what the image had become to her overflowed the ornate gilt frame, spilling into an unattainable significance that left her raw and empty, longing for the comfort of Maebelle's warm body and undemanding adoration. Even the familiar presence of Peter would do.

Pulling herself back into focus, she sat up straighter. Revived by a sip of the inky wine, she tried to listen to Julie explain the intricacies of offering a reward.

Of course you can't wire money or pay anyone who claims to have your dog. Anyone who finds your dog and wants to return it will simply return it. Anyone who wants the money before returning your dog is not likely to have any idea where the dog is. Don't ever send money or use a third party.

Alice wondered what this meant—a courier? iTunes gift card numbers texted to strangers? Western Union? Julie went on.

Beware. There are all sorts out there who have no idea how valuable these animals are. Even if they want the reward—and I know not all of you have offered one yet—these people don't know how to take care of a dog and yet they do know a stud when they see one—if you know what I mean.

She laughed at the innuendo as the rest of them stared at her, politely smiling as if quietly amused even if they were not.

Sebastian just looks like a champ—everyone sees it.

It hadn't occurred to Alice that these dogs were worth money. Julie's Tibetan mastiff was not quite the Tapit of dogs—with his $300,000 stud fee and the highest thoroughbred earnings in North America for five years straight—but in the dog economy Sebastian did quite nicely at $7,000 per mount.

Alice was not a joiner, but she had elected to be part of this group which, it seemed, was even more wrong for her than she'd known. How typical. She wanted Maebelle back for sentimental reasons. Although that was unfair. Calling her attachment to Maebelle sentimental trivialized it, as if her feelings for her dog were automatically less legitimate than her feelings for a human. The loss and longing felt real enough to her. What made the attachment less significant—the species? Of course, Alice knew. It was the reciprocity—or its complexity and quality—that diminished the relationship. Still, there was something to be said for unmediated, unrestrained devotion, whether it was caused by stupidity or not.

Trying not think about the intensity of her attachment and yet vaguely bored, Alice's brain began to trail over the biological conditions that, at least in certain species, determined group coordination: defense. Murmurations of starlings were a response to a predator just over 25% of the time—most often a peregrine falcon, merlin, hawk, or owl looking for a snack.

This didn't tell her much. She wanted to determine the group's evolving dynamic, its purpose and potential. She wanted to break it down, as if doing so would tell her something definitive about the future. Alice considered the costs and benefits of group membership (she might find her dog, but she might be wasting her time); how information was transferred (low, polite speech and understated gestures); how decisions were made (Julie was in charge). Could there be anything more than the mean sum of the parts given the strained manners of this Upper West Side cocktail charade? Was entertaining the fantasy of a higher-level group mind emerging from this ill-sorted assembly just that: a fantasy?

When it came to starlings, the basics of collective action involved seven factors: density, orientation, polarity, nearest neighbor distance, packing fraction, integrated conditional density, and pair distribution. If only she could unravel the dynamics of the room in the same way she analyzed murmurations of starlings as their kinetic formations twisted, turned, swooped, and spun, creating an electrifying effect as a unified flock of ten, several hundred thousand, or even a million. Unlike the off-putting scene before her, the rapidly changing shapes formed by the clouds of birds appeared paranormal. And yet they were nothing more than birds so common they'd long since been identified as an invasive species. It was legal to shoot, trap, poison, or destroy starlings, their nests, eggs, and hatchlings anywhere in the United States.

So what about density? It hardly applied. They'd formed a small group self-selected by geographical location and therefore by class, excluding those who'd lost dogs in Brooklyn, Queens, and the Bronx. Everyone in the room was upper- or upper-middle class by New York standards. The single male in the room, seated to her left, had that patrician effortlessness (never mind his blindingly expensive-looking clothes) that subtly but clearly signaled the presence of both freshly minted and musty bills.

What about the orientation of bodies? They were not all pointing in the same direction the way a shoal of fish do; rather, they formed a neat circle, as a spherical murmuration might at the crucial midpoint of a sharp turn. This critical transition—when the birds swooped around, impossibly coordinated, turning the whole group with such precision it behaved as a single organism—mesmerized Alice every time she'd witnessed it. There was nothing even close to it happening on the twenty-second floor of Central Park West. Their claims to group membership were ultimately so emotionally disparate that the most they definitively shared were their parts in the pulpy, seething mass of humanity that was the life of the city itself.

Suddenly despairing at her ordinary plight, Alice skipped over the complexities of polarity. Humans exhibited some instinct for direction, one that was likely based on a magnetic mechanism in the eye similar to the starling's. Surely Maebelle had the same. Maybe she would find her own way home.

Shaking off a wave of self-pity, Alice considered her nearest neighbor distance (NND). She estimated the distance between herself and Nancy to her left. Nancy's ensemble of silver Birkenstocks, frosty pink toenail polish, white linen pants, and embroidered peasant blouse was roughly sixteen inches away. To her left sat the man with sockless feet in loafers, fine poplin pants in midnight blue revealing a slice of bony, hairy ankle, his razor-sharp shirt with minuscule blue-and-white stripes concealing what appeared to be the hint of a fading winter tan. St. Barts? Guadeloupe? Majorca? He had scooted as far from her as he politely could—right to the edge of the cushion. Perhaps he didn't want to be suggestive? Sitting too close could imply all sorts of things.

Relaxing into her game, Alice shifted her weight toward the back of the sofa, abandoning the awkward edge-of-the-seat position as she settled deep into the plush down that filled the sofa's massive white leather seat cushion. Assessing the group for any outliers, she noted the whole was neatly contained in its circular order. If not that, there was always the packing fraction to consider. It was an amusing, if not particularly useful, consideration. Given the vast glass table and the luxurious depth and breadth of the sofas, the packing fraction would be well above the standard for a murmuration. Alice stared at the oversize low vase of pink and white peonies at the center of the table. Using the flowers as her set point, she tried focusing on the overall shape of the group. It was a turbulent mess, really. They were a loose network. Alice froze for a moment, considering how her smallest movement—reaching forward to grab an hors d'oeuvre—would alter the whole. Julie, the hostess, might lean in to help her reach the tray or a cocktail napkin, thus ending her conversation with Jody, which might have led to an idea that would enable her to find Maebelle. Alice refrained.

The ignorance behind serving red wine in late May, when it was still eighty degrees outside at 6 PM, nibbled at the edge of Alice's good manners until her thoughts were diverted by the prospect of the damage her red wine could inflict on the expensive sofa and white Berber rug should she collide with anyone (or anything). She then sat with the forbidden pleasure she might take in a ghastly spill and the diversion it would offer.

Finally, Julie stopped her talk. People began to chat among themselves. As she considered her next move—whom to talk to as her self-contained silence began to feel conspicuous— she tried to correct her impulse to scoot away from the hint of patchouli wafting her way from Nancy's direction. Why not talk to the man? After all, he looked almost as awkward as she did. Right next to her, he sat staring straight ahead. He'd been nibbling a single morsel of smoked salmon on toast for quite some time. Maybe it had gone off and he was trying to figure out how to politely get rid of it?

Starting the conversation would be an effort. For the past week Alice had done little other than walk the twenty-block radius around her building taping flyers on scaffolding, building entrances, crossing signs, lampposts, subway stairwells, and trees. She'd called the local precinct, veterinary offices, and regional shelters every day. The rest of the time she spent on the web, either monitoring found dogs or updating her posts about Maebelle. She hadn't really talked to anyone. In fact, she'd avoided calling Bette and Emile. She and Peter had agreed not to tell the girls the dog was lost—yet. Why upset them? They were just finished with finals and about to start their prestigious summer internships at the Women's Environmental Network. They had no plans to return to New York before late August.

I'm Alice Foster, she said, haltingly extending her hand and turning her body right to engage what she'd finally determined was an undeniably handsome man. He wasn't facing her, which forced her to speak louder than she would have liked to. What she hoped was a disarming smile was wasted on the air as he continued to stare straight ahead, studying the pattern of dill sprigs on his bitten canapé. After an awful pause during which she feared she'd need to loudly repeat herself, he sensed her eyes on the side of his head and turned with a tiny start.

Oh—hi. He smiled, showing too-white teeth and extending his hand. George McClintock.

Alice, she repeated as she gripped his cool, positively prissy, smooth palm. This wasn't just a man who didn't work in the trades—this was quite possibly a man who didn't work at all. Just carrying a briefcase or suitcase would produce more callous than this George possessed.

I remember you from our chats. You've lost your mutt.

Strictly speaking, Maebelle was a mutt. Although he said it kindly, with a sympathetic warmth that came with a nice crinkle around his fifty-something eyes, she bristled at the word.

Yes. She's a Chihuahua-Dachshund mix. Tiny. Sweet. Aren't they all? Then she recalled that he'd lost a German shepherd. Not tiny and likely not at all sweet. Alice couldn't stand the breed—it always reminded her of Hitler's believed Blondi. That Hitler showed affection for a dog eroded the humanizing value of her relationship with Maebelle. If a man as profoundly evil as Hitler could love a dog and the dog could love him back, then the capacity for loving a dog said nothing about human character, compassion, or morality. Alice liked to think she was more sensitive to dogs than others were, that her bond resulted from her superior ability to understand animals. Of course, charming Rin Tin Tin was also German shepherd, and J. R. Ackerley's sexy companion Tulip had also been a shepherd—or an Alsatian, as the Brits called them. What a strangely wonderful story that was. Alice hoped this man hadn't been quite so handsy with his bitch as Ackerley had so famously been with his.

Yes, well, he said, Slim isn't exactly tiny. But she is sweet. Ninety pounds of devotion last I checked. I miss her like hell.

Ick, thought Alice. *Ninety pounds of devotion*. It sounded like a line someone might use in a Tinder profile. A shame. He really was handsome. What a pleasure it was to admire such a man at close range.

Any luck?

Not really. I had a strange call two days ago. Someone said, I saw a big dog in the park. Brown. Red collar. Just like your poster says. Is there a reward? It was disturbing. Of course I've put up ten thousand dollars. It says so right on the poster. But, as Julie said, nobody is going to call to ask about it. If they have the dog and they're decent, they'll return her and decline the reward. Or, at worst, take it reluctantly. It shouldn't be the first thing they ask.

Yes. Yes. The world is full of creeps. But what can you do, Alice replied politely, unsure of what to do with much of what he'd said. $10,000? Given her offer of $2,000, someone might assume she didn't love Maebelle at all. An awkward pause ensued. Finally, Alice asked, Do you have children? It was not particularly appropriate, but what else could she say? Asking what he did was tantamount to asking how much money he made. Surely that was ruder. Alice suddenly saw him as a serial bachelor, a man who regularly whitened his teeth and kept a giant German shepherd to guard his country house or beach house—or both.

No children. You?

Alice launched into her standard explanation of the twins and her *empty nest*, a phrase she'd grown unbearably tired of but couldn't seem to stop using. It was useful in conveying a great deal of information rapidly: married, children left for college or out in the world, missing them terribly, lonely, marriage going to hell. Now at least he knew she was married.

He listened and then said simply, I'm sorry.

It was an honest response, one that brushed up against the raw truth of many losses. She paused and, looking up from the inside of her wineglass where she'd been staring at flecks of sediment, felt tears begin to drip down her face.

I'm sorry. Sorry. It's been a bit rough, right? Lost dogs and all, she said, trying to laugh off the tears as they continued to fall. She'd been embarrassingly weepy lately. Perimenopause?

Pardon me, she said, and abruptly set her wineglass down and unearthed herself from the depths of the cushion.

She found the bathroom only after startling the maid, who was leaning against the wall in the hallway texting, a grin on her surprisingly animated face. Snapping to attention, she appeared stricken, as if Alice were sure to shout at her.

Excuse me, ma'am. My apologies, she murmured with eyes lowered, leading Alice to the bathroom. Safely inside

behind the locked door, Alice blew her nose and wiped her
eyes with one of the immaculate, crisply ironed linen cloths
on the countertop. The half bath was the size of her bedroom.
The white marble against the glimmering ultramarine mosaic
distracted Alice as she cooled her red eyes and blotchy face with
the damp cloth. Staring critically at herself in the mirror, she
ran her hands through her hair and pulled up her strapless
bra. The fluid fabric of the blue halter top revealed muscular
arms marred by the inevitable loose skin that would soon doom
her to covering her upper arms in polite company. This was
feminine fate—some women managed to keep going longer
than others with relentless weight lifting and the miracle of
brachioplasty, but the time for long sleeves would come. Wiping her nose one last time, she confronted the reality: she had
to go back out and face those fucking people. Christ.

She wanted to slip out the door, down the elevator, and out
past the doormen into the street. She needed a smoke. But the
thought of her empty apartment, absent Maebelle's greeting,
brought on fresh tears. She'd stay. Maybe someone would have
an idea, maybe this failure of group mind would turn itself
around. Stealthy, as if she were winning at hide-and-seek, she
put her hand on the door handle, turning slowly. Through the
crack, Julie's affected voice filtered down the hall. Opening the
door fully, Alice subconsciously closed her eyes as she took a
deep breath to fortify herself for reentry before stepping into
the hall. She opened them on George.

There he stood, just to the side of the bathroom door,
discreetly staring at the opposite wall like a footman in position. For a moment she thought he was waiting to use the
bathroom. Her immediate impulse was to apologize for taking

too long. How embarrassing. But before she could speak he had folded her in his arms, his six feet plus enveloping her body. It was one of those speechless, all-feel hugs—her head forced sideways across his chest, his arms holding her in place with a strength that made her feel smaller and weaker than she was. God it was good. Alice allowed herself to enjoy the experience of letting go, relaxing into his muscular chest for no more than a second or two before she became acutely self-conscious, wondering when he would release her or if she should make the first move to free herself. Of course she was crying again—probably leaving salty tear stains, mascara, and snot on his expensive shirt.

Shhhhhhhh, was all he said, as if she were a child who'd woken from a bad dream. As his arms began to loosen, as Alice began to think she'd better hurry up and extricate herself from him, she realized she could not go back in the room with the other women. She was too far gone, disgusted as much by the entitlement as by her own envy for the excess of money she was sure she could put to better—certainly more tasteful—use. George seemed to intuit at least some of this.

Let's go. You look like you could use a real drink. And with that he brought his mouth close to her ear.

Stay right here.

Silent, the thrill of his warm breath on her ear, she watched him turn decisively toward the living room. From the foyer, it sounded as if everyone in the next room was talking louder than necessary. Maybe it was that 14.5% Napa cabernet? Alice heard the room quiet the moment George spoke.

I'm sorry I can't stay. I've had a promising call about my dog and Alice has kindly agreed to go with me. Thank you,

Julie, for having me—for having us. Alice asked me to thank
you for her.

Oh, please, Julie said. It's nothing. Go. Don't waste any
time. Please call and let us know. I'm dying to know if you get
your baby back.

How sweet of Alice to go with you. I can't imagine how
nervous you must be, another voice chirped to assenting mur-
murs all around.

Well, it's very selfish of me to steal her, but she kindly
agreed. Good night.

A master, thought Alice. Effortless lies piled high for the
sport of it in the course of seconds. Attempting to discreetly
remove what she was certain must be a crust of dried snot from
her nose, she waited with George in silence facing the closed
elevator door, a mild clanking from below indicating its movement toward them. The call light flicked off as the doors slid
silently open on the mirrored interior. While looking straight
ahead, he grazed his hand along the small of her back as if to
guide her, sending a terrifying jolt of fear and pleasure through
her body. They stepped into the elevator, the doors neatly closing out the scene behind them.

Tuesday, May 29

Well, we have to stop for now.

Peter said it at precisely 11:45 AM, his most benevolent smile ready. He hated the look on a patient's face when he broke off a session before it came to a natural stopping point, but it had to be done. In general he took a certain satisfaction in saying the words, underlining as they did his control over the situation. Like the bill, it was an excellent reminder of the transactional nature of what might be mistaken for conversation.

He had just fifteen minutes before his noon appointment to enter *Connection? Broader theme re: neglect—explore* in the patient's file before logging on to the New York State Department of Health website to renew another's patient's Lamictal prescription and return a colleague's call to let her know he would, as a favor, consider accepting a new patient, though he had hardly any holes in his schedule. There was no time to use the common area to boil water for a cup of tea, never mind time to drink the scalding brew before his noon appointment arrived. Peter looked down on doctors who ate or drank in session. A session wasn't teatime.

Sitting down at his desk, he recognized a feeling that must be nerves. Was he nervous about seeing Lisbeth? Not a good sign. What was going on with him lately? He'd had a deeply relaxing weekend in the country without Alice, sleeping late, remaining at the table talking and nibbling bitter chocolate sandwiched between tiny butter cookies and sipping too much Broadbent Port. What a banging headache he'd been rewarded with! He'd endured a five-mile hike on Monday with the whole vaguely hungover group before driving back to the city in the infernal post-holiday traffic. How could 139 miles take six hours?

Among New Yorkers, beating the traffic was a game to lose and participation in the horrors of congestion a misery to bond over. Most of all, talk of traffic was a means to announce one's fabulous destination: a summer house on the Cape, a beach spread in the Hamptons, a family compound in Maine, a farmhouse on Nantucket, an Adirondack camp or a little place in the Berkshires. Actually, Peter had welcomed the traffic the day before. He'd dreaded returning to the empty apartment where Alice would be waiting, droopy and miserable, missing the dog. He would offer what was required— listen, question, sympathize, show solidarity. He was, after all, a professional.

But she'd baffled him. For a moment, sighting her glowing affect as he entered the kitchen, he'd thought she'd recovered Maebelle. Impossible. Besides, the dog had not been there to bark at the sound of his keys in the lock and was nowhere to be seen. And yet she'd appeared lively—the defeated woman he'd seen off on Friday absent. Had she done something to her hair, or was it a new blouse?

Hey. You made it. How was it? she'd said, looking up brightly but not rising from her stool at the kitchen counter. She had been bent over the *Sunday Times Magazine*, a glass of white wine and a pile of crackers on the butcher block just to the side of a glossy full-page Louis Vuitton ad featuring borderline anorexic teenage girls, their limbs spread octopus-like over fancy luggage.

Good, good. Traffic was hell.

He'd put down his racket and overnight bag before opening the refrigerator to fish out a beer. There had been no physical greeting—no hug, no peck on the cheek. He hadn't been gone all that long and she was on the other side of the counter. The moment for a more intimate greeting had passed. She hadn't appeared to expect it or want it herself. Contented in her seat, she'd nibbled one of the super-healthy Swedish cracker breads she always ate—he called them drywall—as she watched him slowly pour a beer into his favorite tumbler.

How are you? No luck? No news?

Not meeting her eye, he'd idly straightened the various sections of the *Times* splayed across the counter in front of him. He'd had to ask about the dog—even though they'd spoken the day before, and he already knew all the answers. She'd looked him in the eye and, averting his gaze, he'd known how perfunctory his questions were.

Nothing.

She'd flipped the flimsy page, briefly distorting the nubile young temptresses into fun house contortions before they disappeared. She'd appeared oddly contented and yet she certainly hadn't been overly chatty. He'd tried again.

You must be exhausted.

He had been the one who'd just gotten out of the car after six hours in traffic, but empathy might open her up. He'd needed to get past the massive wall they'd constructed around the lost dog, one that he could now see had been compounded by his absence. Perhaps he shouldn't have gone?

Not really, she'd finally replied, pushing the magazine aside. I had a quiet weekend. You hungry? Shall we order in?

He'd been perplexed by her mixed mood—uncertain of the lightness of her affect. And yet her self-contained curtness had felt deeply familiar. Alice was practiced at appearances. Being a parent did that to you.

As Alice had explained to him the previous October when, after a month of the girls' absence, he'd pressed her to speak to him about how she was holding up given the evidence that she was not—her hair a tangled wreck, her room piled with dirty clothes, her days spent watching old movies in the den— mothering required mustering the best version of oneself. The ability to be strong and available on command was one of the mixed graces of occupying the role.

Soon after the girls began to talk, Alice had realized that she could break any mood, no matter how dark, to offer herself up to them. She didn't think of herself as generous, and yet it was so easy to give to them. She had wanted them to feel the world was good, to make a home they would never want to leave. But the idyll, such as it was, came at a cost. By pretending to be strong and wise and present she'd almost become all of those things and more. The will involved in inhabiting the imagined role of a good mother had papered over her capacity to experience the world for herself. Over the years she'd wrapped and rewrapped the familiar self-pity and loathing that might otherwise have dominated her mind given the state of her work, marriage, and body, burying it beneath the intricate fabric of their needs. And then they'd left for college. It was in this silent aftermath that she'd contended with the price of losing track of who she was and what she wanted.

Alice had found herself confronted by her least worthy self—while free for the first time in eighteen years to indulge every mood, dark thought, misery, and sadness she harbored. The loneliness the girls' absence brought on curdled emotion, leaving her feeling sour and used. Her doubts about the direction her life had taken had slumbered for years. Alice was back in contact with the self she'd once been while contending with having sacrificed nearly twenty prime years along with her professional ambitions.

Coming to consciousness in the absence of the girls, a ghost of her former vital self was there to meet her in witch's disguise. Feeling as bitter, aged, and sorrowful as she did, how could the dog not have sequestered an outsize place in her emotional life? The dog worshipped her. Alice's very presence in the room was enough to satisfy the animal. What a cowardly emotional refuge she'd chosen.

The lilt of the girls' voices, the perfume of their deodorant and conditioner in the humid bathroom air, the half-eaten apples, yogurt containers, and bowls that rattled with unpopped kernels of corn on the shelf next to the TV were material losses that each time she experienced their absence, freshened Alice's longing for herself in her children's presence. The girls had been enough—enough for her to hold on to a deep, abiding sense of purpose.

They were ordering too much takeout, he thought as he scrolled through Seamless. Their meals together were stilted, put together at the last moment, the impossibility of adjusting to cooking for two demonstrated night after night in quantities of leftovers that sat uneaten, clogging the refrigerator shelves in their hermetically sealed little boxes, the snap-on lids protecting the contents until it was time to take the trash out—at which point they would be unceremoniously dumped. The optimism of keeping leftovers for the requisite three days astonished Peter, but they kept right on doing it.

Later, as he sipped his beer and fiddled with his chop-sticks, he wondered if she'd experienced some sort of epiphany. He'd tried to get past her wall, which persisted over dinner of shrimp dumplings, Dandan noodles, and garlic spinach from Ollie's. Could she be in a better frame of mind? Without finding the dog? He'd felt perplexed and more excluded from her emotional life than ever before. The inexplicable change nattered at him. He hadn't slept well and, with a 7 AM appoint-ment, had risen early.

Unlocking the double doors to his carefully appointed office that morning, he'd felt rough and out of sorts. Peter loved the familiarity of his office, with its soothing watercolor land-scapes, clustered chairs, broad desk, and his prize, a modern Swedish analyst's couch in a muted green tufted velvet—not that his patients ever used it. On most days, the space alone was enough to put him in a balanced, clinical frame of mind. The neutral smell of the room coupled with its sequestered coziness clarified his purpose. Today he couldn't quite shake his unease—was it Alice, the dog, or something over the weekend that had left him distracted?

Waking his computer, he'd read over the notes from the
previous session for his 7 AM. But the post-holiday weeks threw
him off balance; it was Tuesday but felt like Monday. He would
either not see his Monday patients until the following week
or, if necessary, rebook them late or early, or slip them into a
cancellation. Invariably, it was disorderly.

Most of Peter's patients suffered from midlife distress
or some form of emptiness. As a trained analyst of what was
widely known as psychodynamic therapy, he believed working
through these problems had everything to do with a patient's
ability to connect to others. Helping his patients find meaning in their lives while contending with the present and the
past lay at the core of his practice. Nonetheless, if loneliness
described the foundational condition most of his patients presented with, then two words described their symptoms: sadness and anxiety. This intractable pair was continually at play,
one charging the other in dangerous spirals that expanded into
a constellation of needs, wants, indulgences, denials, refusals,
and resistance.

A handful of Peter's patients presented with more than
twenty-first-century malaise. His MD and Big Pharma came
in handy in treating these lifelong mental illnesses. Each one
was driven by an intractable physiological component that
no amount of insight into relationship patterns, attitudes,
behaviors, or habits could address alone. At the moment, three
patients suffered from dysthymia—depressive moods that
came and went but never went away. They responded well to
antidepressants and weekly appointments. Another two manifested symptoms of what Peter loosely viewed as personality
disorders, one of them tinged with an obsessive-compulsive

component that lent itself to paranoid delusion, the other borderline with a heavy serving of narcissism. His longest-standing
patient (fifteen years!) was a woman in her mid-sixties suffering
from an eating disorder that had flared up regularly since her
teens. His most troubling, difficult cases were a schizophrenic
man in his thirties who'd been with him for five years and a
bipolar woman he'd been seeing for just over a year. This last
was Lisbeth Tarkington, his noon appointment.

Just as it was unconscionable to have a favorite child, it
was wrong to have a favorite patient. But sometimes it couldn't
be helped. Lisbeth was young, pretty in a gamine sort of way,
verbally gifted, and afflicted by serious mental illness. She
reminded him of his daughter Bette—both had quick tongues,
self-deprecating manners, and cynical, skeptical minds. In the
year he'd been treating her, there had been no predictable session when she was in the chair. Unlike many of his patients,
whose concerns and the solutions to them required no more
than sensitivity and a sound analytical ability, Lisbeth was an
erratic fast-talker who demanded all of his skill and attention.
Worse, she suffered unrelenting suicidal tendencies when in
depressive phases, which meant any lapses on his part could
have devastating consequences. Her manic phases were char-
acterized by loss of appetite, crazed shopping sprees involving
art, clothing, and jewelry, and sleepless nights spent painting,
cleaning, and watching movies. Fortunately, among her assets
were a sizable trust fund, a feel for form, and a talent for color.
Her art was much more than amateur dabbling—although
he was no expert, she'd shown him a couple of still lifes that
he found at once chilling in their impenetrable precision and
warm thanks to the remarkable quality of light she captured.

The antipsychotic he'd recently prescribed did not seem to be evening her out; he'd have to try something else soon. She was beginning to waste away.

Peter tried not to identify with her. Yet some deep-seated impulse—a classic case of countertransference—compelled him to work harder with her. These sorts of patients were both the worst and best of his profession. He accepted her need to make him essential to her and yet he knew her attachment to him was anything but simple. She'd hinted at sexual fantasies. They came with the job, of course, but in her case he experienced a new sort of danger.

The week before, she'd confessed (late in the session, when most big reveals invariably came out) to a dream of Peter kissing her. He could see her impish, slightly embarrassed demeanor now as she described the surprise of their teeth hitting, the scratch of his stubble on her lips, a vague hint of cinnamon on his tongue. The precision of the details suggested she'd embellished them. Had it been a dream or a confession of a waking fantasy?

It hardly mattered. Both were her fantasies, which was to say the way she told the dream was everything. A dream accrued meaning through the language used to tell it—the narrative of the dream and the dream itself were one and the same. Of course, if Lisbeth's dream were a waking fantasy, as opposed to a memory of sleeping images, then the question of why she'd chosen to tell it as a dream gained significance and would be worth visiting. He hadn't had time to unpack any of this with her the previous week.

When a patient stated his or her attraction to their therapist, it was supposed to be awkward. Peter's training had given him methods to engage and make use of what Freud had quaintly called transference love. Over the years, he'd gotten better at managing the (sometimes) flattering avowals of patients. His standard technique centered on helping the patient explore what it was they were expressing: a desire to be close to him, the need to feel exceptional, the question of whether his office was a space in which they could trust him with their secrets and shameful desires—or something else. It was all pretty standard stuff. Usually, he could draw his patients closer by helping them to distinguish their sexual desires from their underlying wishes for emotional closeness. Allowing them to save face when he rejected them was the key to success. But Lisbeth was different.

After the kissing dream the previous week, he'd been aware of his parched mouth as he spoke. Had he been firm enough when he suggested that her fantasies were normal and important to talk about but that they could never be acted upon as there were essential boundaries proscribing their relationship? Did he believe it? Of course he did, he told himself. He would never transgress the sexual boundary with a patient. As he considered how to handle Lisbeth, he'd become aware of his groin, the stirring of a physical response that was beyond his control. Rising from his chair in alarm, he'd admonished himself to keep her transference and—most of all—his counter-transference under control. But he couldn't stop the memory of his own arousal from at once sickening and fascinating him.

Today he'd managed to get through just five patients and was already shot, sorry he'd scheduled himself no more than a fifteen-minute break before day's end, when the buzzer startled him at 11:58 AM. Collecting himself, Peter buzzed Lisbeth in.

He had two minutes before calling her into his office. For the second time that day he needed to pull himself together. He told himself there wasn't anything terrible about this session. It was just that their previous session, with its unfinished business, nagged at him. And yet he didn't want to bring up her dream unless there happened to be a lengthy silence, in which case he might say, *We never finished our discussion of your dream.* But she was a talker. There would be no silence. She was unlikely to refer to the dream at all, leaving him to wonder if she was embarrassed or emboldened by her confession. He'd have to read her—read them, really. What a mess.

Rising from his desk, he opened the door. There she sat, black leggings encasing long legs zipped into knee-high navy suede boots. She was wearing an oversize black sweater so thin he could see the outline of her gray lace bra beneath it. He made a mental note to record the seductive outfit. As she rose from her chair in the waiting room he imagined running his hand over her shoulder and down her back, stroking gently as he might pet an animal with a lush coat, his hand melting the thread of her sweater to reveal her bare skin beneath. Suddenly aware of the impulse to touch her and how inappropriate the thought was, he checked himself. It wasn't a promising start.

Peter assessed every patient as they walked in the door— affect, posture, eye contact, grooming. They were all tells, clues to the direction of a patient's mood and to what was in store for him during *the hour.* Lisbeth was practically sparkling with energy, her effervescent presence a shock to his system in the room's dull air. The mania that animated her must have been quite something to experience.

Come in.

Attempting to meet her eye, he saw her look at the floor as she walked past him. What he caught was the bittersweet tinge of grapefruit combined with a hint of oily sebum—the smell triggered memories from the girls' childhoods when he'd bury his nose in their fine hair as he tickled and roughhoused with them. It was an intimate smell. Maybe he was wrong. Was she covering up a classic depressive tendency to neglect her grooming with the bright affect and carefully assembled clothing? He'd find out.

Taking his seat opposite her, he waited. The patient spoke first, but she was taking unusually long to begin. Usually her first words were out before he had a chance to settle in his chair with his clipboard on his lap.

I had a shit weekend. If I'd slept any more I'd be dead.

This was rather too provocative for Peter. Never mind her impish smile; any mention of death brought him to attention and all the more so with Lisbeth, who had two solid attempts in her history—thank god not on his watch.

I'm sorry. Tell me.

There isn't much to tell. I watched a ton of old movies . . . Watching movies takes me out of myself. It was as if I was living in the forties and fifties. One after the other, I click *Play* as soon as the closing credits roll, and I'm on to the next.

What did you watch?

Two Greer Garson movies—you know she was plucked from an amateur production? She never set out to be a professional actress. I think if I had to choose a mother from among the leading women of the day, I'd choose her.

And why? Lisbeth's own mother was an alcoholic, a response to her own untreated bipolar, Peter suspected.

Natural warmth. Maybe that's what it is. She just seems like a real woman—even on-screen. I think she'd be steady, ethical, attentive. The only actress I like better is Lauren Bacall. But she's just plain beautiful and mysterious. I wouldn't want Bacall for a mother—that's for sure.

Silence.

Any reason why not?

She'd probably leave her baby on the curb if it didn't match her shoes and purse. I hardly think she suffered any shortage of vanity. But god she has presence. Too bad she traded her career for Bogart. It's almost selfish of her. Think of all the work she gave up, all the pleasure she denied us. But Garson—she's likable. Even in a bad film—I mean *Random Harvest* is silly and implausible. Amnesia is always a cheap way to crank up the drama. But Garson is still worth watching—even when the movie isn't . . .

Peter struggled to stay focused. He hadn't seen *Random Harvest*. In fact, as far as he could recall, he only knew Garson as the saintly housewife in *Mrs. Miniver*. He'd seen it with Alice at Film Forum. They'd actually kissed during the movie—that was how long ago it was. Kissing Alice had grown impossible. Even kissing her in bed if they were ever to occupy one together again felt strange and awkward. They hadn't kissed properly, hadn't really had a taste of one another, in three or four years. Peter then abruptly realized Lisbeth had been talking, and he'd been thinking about kissing his wife—in front of a patient who'd recently expressed a fantasy of kissing him. *Keep it together, Peter*, he'd scratched in the margin of his notes for the day next to *Lisbeth Tarkington. 5/29. Slept too much. Hair dirty, dressed seductively. Death. Watched movies—Greer Garson.*

I like *Desire Me* a lot. The plot's so twisted. Seen it?

No. Never have.

He should have asked her to tell him more about why she liked that film in particular, let her expand her thoughts and associations about mothers, but he couldn't bring himself to do it. *Desire Me*. He was pretty sure she'd plucked out that film by title to flirt. He wouldn't put it past her. Skipping over the conversation about the film was his first instinct—he hated feeling manipulated by a patient. And yet this was his chance to bring up the awkwardness of the previous week and to recover from his own reverie about Alice.

Sometimes, despite the $400 per hour he earned for each forty-five-minute increment, he felt underpaid. Forgetting a key piece of information was unforgivable—spouses' and partners' names, places of birth, status of parents, professions, sex lives, troubles at work, fears, traumas, aspirations, betrayals, medications, dosages, dreams, neighborhoods, pets, drinking and eating habits, sleep patterns, sibling-and-parent dynamics, names of children, financial status, anecdotes—it never ended. Fortunately, his memory was excellent. He couldn't have done his job without the ability to encapsulate every detail of each patient's life into a meme that animated the moment the patient walked into his office.

It's too bad Garson is forced to play a naive puppy, Lisbeth continued. And the melodrama is a bit much. But I guess that's what I love about classic film. It's unreal—so removed from the way we live now. We never question Greer's integrity. When she falls for Renaud, we know it's a mistake. He's a cad and a trickster, but her innocence and goodwill are palpable. What I still can't quite sort out is the opening.

When is it supposed to take place? She's clearly with Renaud the impostor when she speaks to the doctor, but at what point do they have the conversation? There she is in the office with the grand old doctor in his white coat. He says, *You're sick but not in the way you think.* I wish some doctor would say something like that to me . . . *You'd die rather than face it.* And then she confesses to him: *Our life together has no meaning,* and I'm thinking, *what the hell are you doing then? Why don't you just—*

There it was again. Death. And sex. She might as well have been addressing him directly when she said, *I wish someone would say that to me.* He needed to get past the shield of the film criticism—ask her what she would imagine he would say to her if he were to speak in direct, diagnostic terms. This sort of abstract talk was a defense. Lisbeth was covering the discomfort of being in his presence with a thinly veiled conversation about the film's treatment of marriage, infidelity, betrayal, innocence, and most of all, his way of treating her. She was criticizing his treatment of her illness, his indifference and neglect. Although Peter didn't realize it, Lisbeth was also expressing a fantasy that he cheat on his wife. And not just through Garson in *Desire Me,* but also through the repressed memory and expression of true love in *Random Harvest.*

What Peter did see was the misdirection. When it occurred in session, it was incumbent on him to steer the patient back to him or herself—back to the two people in the room and what was happening in what was called *the in-betweenness* of therapist and patient. Otherwise known as the here and now. *Here and now.* It was his mantra whenever he wasn't sure what to say to a patient.

She was using the movies to talk about herself. And in turn, wasn't he, too, thinking about himself as he considered evading or engaging Lisbeth's complaints, desires, longing, and explicit sexual fantasies? What to say next? It was impossible to properly untangle in the immediacy of the moment, but he needed to say something. And he needed to say the right thing—or at least not the wrong thing.

I also rewatched *The Silence of the Lambs*. God, I love that movie. Why didn't Demme make anything else nearly as good? I love how she uses the dog to save herself. Her voice shaking: *Here, Precious. C'mon, girl. Precious.* And then she tries to whistle to the dog but her lips are so chapped she can't make any sound come out.

Lisbeth then pursed her own lips and emitted a low whistle. She then cringed, shaking her head as if physically shrugging off the memory of the scene's horror would make it go away.

Was there a reason you chose to watch *The Silence of the Lambs* again and bring it up here, now?

He hadn't addressed the Garson films, but at least he was back in the present, bringing her back in the room. The psychiatrist as predator. The psychiatrist eating—literally consuming—his patients. Lisbeth was going dark, taking him to her fears of his influence over her, taking him right to the meaty center of the ontological dangers of the psychotherapeutic process. At least he'd seen the movie. All shrinks knew Hannibal Lecter's unforgettable line about the man whose head Clarice Starling discovers in the storage unit: *Best thing for him really. His therapy was going nowhere.* He could engage with Lisbeth intelligently. But only if he were using it to move them beyond the movies and back to the present moment in the room.

Whatever sort of good or bad object he was to her—and he was certain there was plenty of bad in this stew of fantasies, fears, and transference love—he needed to straighten himself out. He couldn't afford to lose his technique.

Tuesday, May 29

The irrational fear that Peter could see her thoughts had Alice dissimulating. She'd stared, unseeing, at the *Times* to avoid his gaze. The facts that had gone unsaid since his return from the country pulsed through her body in reckless circuits of pain and wonder. Alice feared the shift represented a termination, as if she'd come to the end of a version of herself. Had she arrived at the end of a phase of her relationship with Peter and opened up something dangerous and unfamiliar?

From the time Peter walked in the door after his weekend away, all he had talked about was Maebelle—as if Alice's entire existence were defined by the lost dog. Of course this was in a way true, thought Alice. He wasn't really wrong. This was not to say she'd ceased to project how miserable the animal must be without her, how much the dog longed for her. The anxiety-laden guilt this left her with was unbearable; Alice preferred to believe Maebelle dead than to inhabit her suffering—not just lonely but hungry, thirsty, and possibly in physical pain. The loss of Maebelle that had been raw on Friday when Peter left was, on Tuesday morning, a wound that almost appeared to have healed but in fact continued to fester beneath the eschar. Alice wondered if grief had poisoned her blood, intoxicating her judgment and sense. She feared she'd forever lost a claim on her former, familiar self.

Giddy with the shock of her isolation from Peter given all that had happened in between, she'd responded effortlessly to his inquiry about her weekend. She'd hardly known what she said as she'd watched him go through his stale shrink routine of sympathetic questions, exhibitions of empathy and concern.

I am sorry, Alice.

And then a meaningless litany: Tell me about how you're feeling; I was hoping you'd have some news; you've done everything possible; you really love her; animals have played a significant role in your emotional life since you were a child; you miss her terribly, I know; I miss her, too; is there anything, anything at all, I can . . .

How tiresome it was to watch him pull out his banal bag of analytic tricks. She played along, but just for once it would have been nice if he could have left his training at the office. She wanted to remind him he wasn't in session—he didn't have to elicit her emotion, unravel her past, and offer the ideal springboard for her emotional response. He could be a husband, not a doctor. The idea that he'd failed her—rather than she him—comforted her. Yes, she thought victoriously. He wasn't connecting. What did she expect from him after all those hours listening and remaining at a remove, a transparent vessel for his patients? It wasn't her fault he'd spoiled his own capacity to engage in a mutual, intellectually and emotionally honest relationship.

Peter had left the apartment early, well before she'd risen. The residue of his hunger: milk sweating on the counter, dark crumbs like lost ants scattered around the toaster, the tiny loaf of butter gouged, and a smear of overpriced blueberry jam that had worked its pigment into the butcher block. The jam, with its hand-stamped label and raffia bow, had been a token gift from the Berkshires—for her. It had inked the newspaper, traces of it leaving a sticky film on the tips of Alice's fingers. She rinsed her hands. The stacked gold rings on her wedding finger flashed wet under the faucet, exotic against the spectacle of ropey veins and sharp metacarpal bones defining the backs of her hands—a messy map of the freeways somewhere near LAX. She attacked the jam on the counter with the rough green side of the sponge. Scrubbing the surface raw, she created a pale irregular circle that stood out in contrast to the worn, slightly greasy maple surrounding it.

Up until a week ago, she would have given a low whistle and said in her most chipper, singsong dog voice: *Pee-pee?* Maebelle never needed to be called, really. She trailed Alice around the apartment, sniffing this and that but ultimately straying no farther than a horsefly on a hair leash. Alice voiced the inane call only to elicit the excitement of a walk, to take pleasure in Maebelle's enthusiasm at the ritual of going out to inspect the redolent urban wilderness.

Alice instead did what she'd done every day since Maebelle's disappearance: she took a walk without her for the purpose of hoping, somehow, to happen upon her—even to happen upon her body, which would by now have decomposed somewhat—and to sneak a cigarette. Entering on 96th she headed toward West End Ave, examining every dog bearing any resemblance to Maebelle whether the beasts were tucked into greasy sleeping bags next to begging cups on the sidewalk or trotting at the ends of a calfskin leashes. She scrutinized the homeless because they were among the least wired people in the city. If they found Maebelle wandering, they might have limited access to the internet's miraculous lost-and-found dog networks or even to a phone. Besides, wouldn't a dog as becoming and lovable as Maebelle be almost impossible for a person who had lost everything to pass up?

Even before losing Maebelle, Alice had instinctively broken her stride at the sight of a man or woman living on the street with a cat or dog. She frequently bought a coffee and a buttered roll for a woman with a tabby who had long frequented a doorway on 92nd Street. Alice was concerned; she hadn't seen her in weeks. Of course, a position on the sidewalk offered little safety, especially for a woman. The unhappy piles of possessions—backpacks, blankets, suitcases, and invariably plastic bags filled with unnamed treasure—signaled the precious remains of domesticity gone horribly awry. People with pets appeared more secure to Alice, as if the comfort of a dog or cat might ground them, magically turning a stretch of sidewalk into a home. Wasn't a pet the last vestige of family? The power to care for another being mattered. In the absence of other intimacy and comfort, a pet might command all of one's need for love and affection. That was something.

But there were no dogs to be found, prosperous or impoverished, dead or alive. Returning to her apartment, Alice confronted what she'd walked out to escape: the disorderly space. She couldn't be bothered to put the dishes in the dishwasher, take down the garbage, or run a load of wash. So she opened her laptop and repeated the routine she'd followed every morning since Maebelle had gone missing: searching Petfinder for newly posted small dogs available for adoption, looking for responses to her lost dog queries on the various Facebook pages, posting a fresh query on Maebelle's personal Facebook page. She then called the precinct, the vet, and the Manhattan Animal Care Center on 110th Street. Exhausted and depressed by the thought of Maebelle, she ignored the chatty conversations between members of the lost dog association and made herself another latte. Hopeless.

She had no distinct memory of getting to the bar where she'd sat with George for hours drinking cocktails while sharing, among other things, a heaping plate of shoestring fries they'd dipped in a lemony, pepper-flecked mayonnaise. It had been the first really hot evening of summer, one of those days when the anticipated cool of night never arrives. The too-hip restaurant had opened its levered glass doors to the sidewalk, placing tables and chairs behind a cordon of tall, freshly whitewashed planters. Alice could picture the flowers. They'd been nothing more than seedlings, really, black dirt tentatively holding trembling zinnia stems upright despite the weight of their green-button buds that within weeks would be a brilliant radial arrangement of perfect candy-colored petals.

Her perpetually fermenting class rage had led her to read George all wrong. He wasn't simply a rich playboy, despite his too-fine clothes, shoes, and teeth. He was a rich infectious disease specialist. What was it with her and doctors, she wondered. It was as if she could spot them from afar—and they her. Rather than drinking through and past the mundane and

likely diminishing tales of inadequate parents, disappointing
spouses, lonely childhoods, and nostalgic college and grad
school years, they abstained from personal history. It was as
if they'd met anonymously abroad, knowing that what passed
between them was present tense and need not be encumbered
by the identities they'd acquired any more than by their future
prospects. There'd been no talk of lost dogs. Alice was liberated
to inhabit herself as she pleased.

Tell me about your work.

They were the first words he'd spoken once they'd found
their seats. It was a neutral question intended to prevent any
further discharge of distressing tears after their rapid exit. Alice
knew crying women were onerous to men—even sensitive men
who hugged distressed women on impulse. Not a word had
been said as the elevator descended 88 Central Park West, nor
on the walk down Amsterdam Avenue. He'd guided her surely,
clearly with a destination in mind, to the bustling restaurant.
They managed to find two open stools at a quiet corner of the
bar. She'd again felt the wickedly suggestive pressure of his
hand, barely perceptible on her back as she found her seat. She
could feel her hot cheeks and feared that anxiety and excitement
made her appear febrile.

I'm a biophysicist.

She had not apologized or otherwise equivocated about
the state of her career. It was a habit she had: apologizing for
what she'd become in her own mind, even though to others
she was shockingly well educated and accomplished.

I'm at work on flock dynamics. The phenomenon I
study is known as scale-free correlation. This isn't, of course,
limited to biology. In fact, the closest correlations to starling

flock patterns are in the broader literature of criticality. This includes crystal formation and avalanches—in other words, stable systems poised on the brink of dynamic change. When so poised at a moment of criticality, the system itself has the capacity for near-instantaneous transformation, often without a single catalyst.

Alice had then paused to study George's response while offering an inquisitive smile. She'd continued. Sorry. Did any of that make sense? It's really just the study of how birds communicate in large flocks called murmurations. Being critical means the system is poised to respond to internal and external perturbation—which for starlings is usually a raptor—

Alice had then stopped her explanation midsentence with a laugh—What? What's funny? She'd suddenly felt rather pretty. Girlishly tucking a strand of hair behind her left ear, she'd studied the captivating grin on George's handsome, tanned face, a grin so wide his teeth showed their full polished glory.

I'm laughing, he'd said, looking hard into her eyes without blinking, because you wouldn't believe what I do.

What do you mean?

I work in infectious disease. My field involves critical systems—not starlings. Bacteria are my babies. I'm sure you're familiar with the explosion of work on biofilms—matrices of bacteria that form into sheets after swirling in unison. They behave, not unlike your murmurations, as a single organism. They're getting all sorts of attention because antibiotics can't penetrate biofilms the way they can individual bacteria—likely just as a hawk or peregrine can't attack a murmuration the way it can easily pick off an individual bird. Biofilms offer opportunities and pressing challenges to the treatment of antibiotic

resistant infection. On the flip side, of course, they're impli-
cated in metastasis, particularly when the spread of cancerous
cells occurs . . .

He'd talked fast, eyes alight in a way that was at odds with
the dullness she'd encountered just thirty minutes before as
he stared stoically at his canapé. It was difficult to believe they
belonged to the same man. Alice coveted the gray-blue of his
irises, imagining it as yarn she could turn into what would
surely be her most desirable sweater.

What can I get you? the mere girl of a bartender had asked,
indelicately, interrupting the flow of talk. Alice had observed her
eyeing George from beneath her artfully done false eyelashes.
She'd then placed two menus on the bar.

I need something fresh after that heavy red wine. You?
George said, passing her one of the cream-colored, fine-paper
menus.

Absolutely, she'd replied, trying to focus long enough to
decipher the handwritten descriptions next to the outlandish
titles of the cocktails on the menu before her: Gin-Gin Mule,
Firefly, Classic Chelsea Sour, Mrs. Dalloway, Old-Fashioned
Girl, Paloma.

What do you say to a Mrs. Dalloway? Then he'd added,
in a Howard Cosell–selling-hemorrhoid-cream voice: Refreshing cucumber-mint muddle, Sapphire gin, and house-made
lime-infused seltzer. Returning to his normal voice he added,
It thinks quite a lot of itself but sounds refreshing.

Perfect, she'd replied, relieved to be free of the decision
and genuinely pleased with the choice. The combination of
cucumber, gin, and mint—so compatible it was almost one fla-
vor. And then there was the lonely, perceptive woman behind it.

What would the tea-drinking Woolf have thought of a gin drink named after her? Or did Woolf actually take a stiff drink now and again? Alice couldn't remember—or didn't know. A flash of Clarissa Dalloway's memory of daring to kiss Sally Seton and how it left her with *something infinitely precious* had, at that moment, inspired Alice with the confidence to open herself up, to fearlessly relax into the present moment—maybe to try embracing the surprising flutter of pleasure she'd experienced in response to a stranger's hand on her back.

The bartender had turned, responding to the subtlest flick of George's hand, as if she'd been watching, awaiting his command. Alice could hardly blame her.

What can I get you?

Two Mrs. Dalloways, please. And an order of *boquerones*.

He'd pronounced *boquerones* with a bit more Spanish flair than necessary, but he'd been polite and best of all he had not so much as glanced at the bartender's kittenish lean, which had caused her cleavage to spill forward as if it, too, were an ordinary offering George might like to order up.

Alice had again tried to breathe and absorb the situation. She'd had to ignore the man buns, Brooklyn beards, and skinny, skinny girls whose linen short shorts and platform wedges broadcast legs she might once have thought not quite as comely as her own. *Slow down*, she'd told herself. She was at a bar with a man whose command over her had been a necessity as she tried to escape Julie's apartment. Now that command felt less necessary, and yet she'd already allowed him the lead. Worse, she'd relinquished herself to it—her passivity inviting him to chaperone her as he selected the restaurant, seats, drinks, and food. She'd felt like a girl. To be taken in hand as George had taken her had left Alice with a singular, irresistible impulse: to submit.

Everything with Peter was a negotiation. Where to go, when to go, where to sit—it never ended. And then there was the conversation, which, as they'd aged into each other, became a task she and Peter willingly and (mostly success-fully) engaged. But it took a concerted effort. If either of them were distracted, irritable, or tired, the conversation lagged or, worse, threatened to wander into dangerous zones where long-standing disagreements flared up. Spoiling an evening was as effortless as downing a bad oyster.

The bartender had returned and again tried to catch George's eye as she landed the tall, frosty cocktails. No go.

To phase transitions, Alice had said, raising her drink. The clink as they touched glasses felt conspiratorial. As Alice inelegantly removed the paper napkin from the bottom of her glass where it had dangled through the clink and first sip, George had explained the mechanics of a promising new experimental model. She'd listened, taking in the effortless efficiency of his explanations. His goal was to identify the source of cells' signaling mechanisms. It was, after all, com-munication that enabled them to form collective states. Alice was struck by the uncanny similarity to her main concern—how starlings transmitted information about their position in real time. He'd gotten a bit carried away explaining an exciting success using biopolymeric films for the delivery of the antibiotic levofloxacin. Alice had drifted then, studying his refined features more than listening as he delved into films modified with high methoxylated pectin capable of incorporat-ing an antibiotic payload of 6.23 mg g-1, perfectly adequate to eradicate the *Staphylococcus aureus* used in the samples. But for the most part, with the fluency of enthusiastic colleagues privileged to work in fields yielding facts previously unknown to science, they'd entangled ideas from their respective areas of expertise in uneven rushes, their common language interspersed with socially lubricating laughter.

After covering the signal-processing speeds and low noise that makes the synchronous movement of birds and bacteria possible, they'd dissected the challenges of gathering accurate data from various models. Birds posed experimental difficulties bacteria did not—even if they rewarded the observer with dramatic displays. His experiments, on the other hand, were easy to control and in truth, as Alice knew from her grad work, had their own colorful, minute elegance that could be seen on a slide as a chaotic swarm that, with adequate density, also became synchronized oscillations. Differences aside, bacteria and starlings were irresistibly analogous.

By their third Mrs. Dalloway, Alice was pleasantly high. They'd arrived at why and how collective behaviors exist and how to best study emergence. They'd disagreed over the degree to which humans exhibited and benefited from collective behaviors, the value of collective intelligence, the roles of epistemic democracy in a world leaning toward dictators, and the value of AI on human evolution. They'd parsed the difference between slime molds, swarms of honey bees, stock exchanges, the internet, schools of sardines, and predictive logarithms on Amazon. Alice had suggested that the brain's neurons constituted the ultimate example of the power of collective behavior. They'd jostled for some time over active matter. Was collective action inherent in matter itself?

The evening stripped Alice of her grief and malaise. It was as if she'd had a Silkwood shower, leaving behind the toxicity of her grief, anger at Peter, and raw longing for the presence of her girls. When she'd reluctantly arrived at Julie's apartment for the lost dog association meeting, Alice couldn't have predicted the result. Her mind had gotten her in trouble. George's handsomeness was a cheap bonus by any standard. But the mind she encountered—that was irresistible, which was why, by the end of the evening, she'd wanted to erase the margins between them by hazarding more of him. Her desire to join minds had reduced itself to its most literal form as she visualized the tactile reality of his lengthy, muscular form. In the end, it was always about energy and matter.

Alice never planned to be unfaithful to Peter, whatever their limitations and problems. Her life with him was stifling, but it was all she'd known for well over twenty years. Everything she valued, they shared. Except, of course, their respective fields. And that was how George had made his inroad. That fissure, that gap between her work and Peter's, was precisely how he'd escaped the censure of tradition and habit that kept her sealed off and loyal to Peter—to her family. How could she have known? The conversation, exciting beyond any she'd had in years, consumed every sense. The fantasy of intellectual sympathy, of being seen as George's worthy opponent and peer, was too potent to resist.

They'd closed the bar. Each, Alice sensed, had been putting off the decisive movement of entering the dark anonymity of the street, away from the protective light and conventional manners of the bar. Delay had allowed her time to consider escaping once she'd realized what she'd allowed herself to want. Drugged by their conversation and tipsy from drink, she'd felt the compulsion to hold, smell, taste, and entangle herself fully with George overwhelm her. She'd wanted to fuck him—strictly speaking, she'd wanted him to fuck her. That was the crude, simple truth of it.

She had tried to talk herself out of it. *Don't*, she'd thought. *This is poison.* Not worth it. She didn't want to become a divorce cliché—confronting the wounded look on Peter's kind face when she confessed. Oh god. And the girls. Knowing that they might picture her having sex with a man they'd never met. Somehow, the sex of the parents who created you doesn't count as sex; copulation tamed by reproductive history—or something like that. But another man? The two of them knowing she'd wounded their gentle father, effectively blasting apart their family for what would appear to them and to Peter as nothing more than the cheapest, most self-indulgent sexual thrill. Surely there was truth in that accusation.

No. That hadn't been it—not all of it. As physical, as sexual, as her desire undeniably was, what she'd experienced at the chilling moment of decision couldn't be reduced to lust. Through George she'd located a shred of her former self. He'd seen and reflected herself back to her as Alice—the geeky girl who'd rather study than party, the girl who lost track of time in the lab, the girl who flew to Rome, staying alone for weeks in an unheated youth hostel in January near the Piazza Trilussa to observe and film the massive murmurations over that ancient, noble city. The girl who loved nothing better than data.

None of what she'd chosen was against Peter. But then, maybe it was, and it was simply nicer to think it wasn't. She wanted to believe she'd made her choice to leave the bar with

George in an effort to save herself; she'd even managed to convince herself that walking to the hotel with him, standing there in the dazzling lobby while he registered and paid, opening the door to the splendid luxury of an anonymous bed to share with this stranger, had never really been a choice. It just was.

But sitting in their familiar kitchen, with Maebelle lost in the world, Peter ensconced in his office on 82nd Street engaged in intimate conversation with strangers, her girls sleeping in their Durant Avenue dorm rooms far off in California, where it was not yet dawn—she was alone with complicated truths. Alice wished she could stop tending her orderly life—the one she wasn't sure she wanted anymore—but she couldn't quite shake the feel of the bed at the Mandarin.

Now she had to decide if the night and George himself were to become sordid secrets she'd force herself to tell. Must she put them out in the world to avoid becoming (in nobody's mind but her own) a liar? Must she ruthlessly lance the ugliness of pretending to be something she was not—transparent, truthful—to preserve herself? Or did preserving herself involve preserving the truth, keeping it as her own. As Mrs. Dalloway recognized, *she felt that she had been given a present, wrapped up, and told just to keep, not to look at it.*

Alice wasn't sure she had the constitution to keep it and herself in one piece. She had no experience with outsize secrets, and this one was much more significant than anything she'd had to contend with before. Alice reminded herself that her body belonged to her; the current sleeping arrangements underlined this fact. She'd had a refresher on the rough

intimacy of sexual pleasure. It was a negotiated physical trans-
action involving sweat, semen, saliva, and other, unknowable,
unnameable, body fluids. Good sex was sticky, but it was also
emotional. She'd almost forgotten.

Perhaps she could make George into an insignificant
thing that simply *was*. A fragment of the past that merited no
further attention. The easiest and the most cowardly course,
but also perhaps the best, was to allow the secret to run its
course internally, silently dissipating the way a newly plowed
snowbank, at first tall and magnificently textured with clumps
and crests, over time grows soft and round only eventually to
shrink into a crust of icy crystals before they, too, are reduced
to water.

There was no question—at least she refused to allow herself to think there was—of seeing George again. As simultaneously appalling and wonderful as holding on to the secret
was, repeating it would turn an indiscretion into *having an
affair*. It would then be as sordid as it sounded. *Fling* had a
much gentler ring to it, if a bit tacky.

She would keep it sacrosanct, unsullied by accusations
and couple's therapy and the nauseating analysis of what
she'd done and why and who she'd hurt and all the tedious
rest of it. She felt it within the realm of the possible to keep
the anomaly to herself, to keep *the radiance*. As her secret it
could boost her, fluff her up, spirit her to survive. If she chose
silence, the memory could remain encapsulated, entombed
deep in her private self as a discrete event that, by some dev-
ilish shift in the warp of time, didn't belong to her life with
Peter. She needed the vast reservoir of pleasure to slowly,
tenderly draw down.

Moving from the kitchen to the living room, Alice sank into her favorite armchair. Still clad in nothing more than a flimsy camisole and pajama shorts, closing her eyes, she felt the soft velvet of the chair's fabric on the back of her bare thighs. She knew it well; it was the color of the pigeons' underbellies that cooed and strutted, purposeful as car salesmen, on the window ledges around the apartment. Thinking of the plebeian birds, content to pass their days waiting for trash to fall their way on the streets of the city, she visualized the masses of starlings feeding in the marshes on stopover as they migrated north over Denmark. She imagined herself back in Jutland at dusk, bundled in her puffy down jacket and black watch cap, staring up at the sky to witness one more *sort sol*. Tens of thousands—even millions—of birds doing what birds do in the wild: feeding, shitting, bickering, preening, fighting, breeding. Messy and raucous, she can almost hear their sharp cries fill the air with a shock of sound that's the opposite of static. Abruptly, the moment impossible to pin, they transition from disorder to orderly flow, the shape and grace of their movements closer to liquid, smoke, or gas than to the squawking flesh, feather, beak, and bone of *Sturnus vulgaris*. The universe is their audience as they twist, fold, roll, explode, bend, ripple, and undulate.

Their collective movement is beautiful, which is to say their uncanny symmetry communicates fear—or at least an unsettling sense of powerful order. What makes the flock's movements compelling? Alice sees them in her mind, both a memory and a production, as the angled light of the setting sun reflects off millions of feathers covering wings, breasts, and tails. Together their mass casts a shadow over the land, darkening the space beneath them. Black sun: *sort sol*.

Alice has worked for twenty years to grasp the unseen intelligence of the flock in motion. But even if she can't, she can borrow from it—for in motion the birds become a single noun: *it*. And no, not just a name of the action: murmuration. The whole system demands a name that is its own simple noun designating what species the mass becomes as one, because when the organism breaks into individual parts, it dies. It is a time-and-place-specific creature that is never twice the same.

After the birds settle, the *sort sol* is no longer an effect the birds have created with their mass; it becomes a natural, inevitable effect of the earth's rotation. The sky darkens. Time to sleep. It's Tuesday morning in New York, but Alice is deeply tired. In trees, the birds cover the branches, roosting in clusters for safety and warmth. But before they take flight at dawn, a tree housing five thousand starlings disturbs the sight as the density of their bodies reshapes the symmetry of each branch. The scale reads wrong. From afar the birds appear as tiny bumps—an infestation of aphids on a doomed houseplant. Woe to any blossom, bug, or blade of grass beneath; it will be slick with guano by sunup.

Saturday, June 16

Peter: *Please everyone send me a picture of what you are looking at right now.* Above the message was a picture of the wildly eclectic posters, playbills, photographs, and books that defined Peter's home office. In the foreground was a half-eaten pastrami sandwich, the vivid yellow mustard visible on the butcher paper.

The family chat included Bette, Emile, Alice, and Peter, a post-phone-call-era cooperative effort that required nothing more than simple expressions of enthusiasm and the occasional question. How was the movie? Did you get the package? How are your classes? Did the internship come through? The query for what each one of them was looking at that very moment was Peter's remarkable way of dipping into the texture of each of their lives, no matter where they were. He'd been doing it for years.

Everyone always responded. Bette and Emile were old enough to take the time to offer their lonely parents news, photos, and enthusiasm; they were old enough to worry about them, beginning the gradual shift to their old age when all they would do is worry. For now, the slightest germ of this reversal manifested itself.

Alice: *Urban gardening!* Attached was a photo of her black rabbit's foot fern, airy green on top with hairy tendrils encasing the terra-cotta pot as if to strangle it.

The texts were a thin facsimile of the family dynamic. Alice played second to Peter's newsy, more frequent reports. Bette cracked sarcastic comments. Emile chimed in with sweet expressions of missing them all. Alice, too often, stood aside and enjoyed the back-and-forth while offering the occasional photograph. None of the tensions of being in one another's presence found their way into the texts, or if they did it was as a subdued undercurrent expressive of long-formed relationship dynamics and the stereotypes families specialize in. The group text worked as an idealized script representing the family as a unified, mutually supportive unit that fed off a particular form of intimacy. Most of their lives weren't in the texts—by their very nature they were truncated snippets or reflexive expressions of love and longing. Money business, boyfriend troubles, worries about any one of the group members—these realities were confined to individual texts and phone calls.

Because its character depended on happy chatter, ever since Maebelle's disappearance Peter and Alice had engaged the group less frequently, the necessary silence resting in a cool void behind the cheerful photos of meals and favorite places feeling disingenuous. Worse, Alice realized just how many of the photos she shared had featured the adorable, eminently photogenic Maebelle.

Twenty minutes later.

Emile: *A bonanza of solar panels.* The photo showed massive stacks of solar panels in dull brown boxes printed with a ●.

Alice: *Whoa! Capture that California sun.* ♥

Bette: *Hey, I'm here too! Attention hog.* (A virtually identical photo followed.)

Emile: 👄 👄 👄

Peter: *So impressive—BOTH of you!*
👊 👊 👊 👊

Alice put her phone down. The banal exchange was at once deeply sad and extraordinarily satisfying. As if she were suffering from PTSD, the images of George's bare thighs, muscular arms, smooth pectorals, and naked buttocks played and replayed themselves in her mind as she sprayed the giant ficus in the living room. The interior branches were looking barren and stark, but partially unfurled leaves, tender and delicate as rice paper on the tips of the outer branches, reassured her. Gathering crispy dead leaves curled in on themselves in the dense interior of its branches, she relived the thrill of him standing behind her in the hotel elevator, his hand encircling her from behind to find the button of her jeans, deftly unclasping it with one hand and then moving beneath her underwear to find the mat of hair covering her pubic bone. Deadheading the geranium, she replayed the movement of his long, smooth fingers as they slid lower, stopping at the surprisingly wet folds of her vagina, dipping in briefly only to retreat to the dainty protuberance of her clit. Nature had been good to women; it was the simplest pleasure button. Alice replayed the rush she'd experienced on the way up to the penthouse, her breath catching and her ears popping as he toyed with her. She'd tried not to make a noise as he settled into a gentle but unmistakably vigorous motion.

Refilling the watering can, she entered her own room to water the ferns, pilea, jade, bay, and rubber tree. She shuddered at how wrong of her it was to take pleasure in the memory of her night with George. The family group text was a distillation of what she risked—she would lose access to it. No, she would blow it to pieces. It was a fragile collective. Never again would she be part of this tiny ecosystem that was her family. By not telling Peter, perhaps she could make it less real. So far, all the memory had done was grow into an obsessively repeated reel crowding her mind, unbidden, the way a vision of Peter or the girls in a car wreck did—impossible to contain because attempting to block it out only made the image recur.

The anxiety over the repetition of the sexual images left her feeling sullied and, far too frequently, aroused. Confusingly, the sex she'd had with George and the memory of it made her more attracted to Peter, and yet she was deeply afraid to initiate sex with him. It had been two years since they'd fucked, and it had been less than spectacular. Alice had turned over after the encounter feeling she'd survived something that could have gone worse. The stakes were too high when sex was so infrequent. Without any regular sexual commerce, fucking became a litmus test of their love and compatibility. Could they still make each other come? What if they failed? The disaster of not completing the act, of having bad sex—whatever that was—hung over them both. By avoiding sex they elided the blunt reality that they'd lost the ability to excite each other and, beneath that the rough truth, that they were no longer attracted to one another.

As she misted the maidenhair fern, she considered what bad sex was. Wasn't being sexually stimulated by someone a function of some animal instinct more than an indication of love? She'd been overwhelmed by desire for George, but she didn't love him. Was the whole concept of bad sex she and Peter had internalized a crude distillation of the Western romantic narrative? It was a story obsessed with authenticity, a reified ideal of dedicated couples from Penelope and Odysseus to Antony and Cleopatra.

Alice realized that she occupied the feminine position, a position defined by waiting—as it was in so many iconic romantic stories: *Romeo and Juliet, Sleeping Beauty, Cinderella, Rapunzel.* But waiting for what? If anything, Alice was waiting for acceptance. Peter wasn't happy with her. Had that been what was so magical about George? George didn't know her well enough to yearn for a better version. To him, she simply *was,* and he was curious to know her, to appreciate her in her present form. Were Peter's demands for elements of her former self a function of her failures? Peter seemed incapable of the generosity and self-assurance to accept her as she was in the present. Maybe the solution when it came to sex was to leave their complicated expectations, disappointments, memories, resentments, and all the rest out of the bed. If they treated each other's bodies as nothing more than opportunities for pleasure, they'd have better success—or at least more fun.

The whole mess made her feel tender toward Peter, as if she now owed him greater consideration given the peril she had put herself and, by extension, them in. The organism that made a whole from its parts was fractured by the loss of Maebelle and by the peeling away of the girls. It couldn't withstand another blow. And yet she'd put the whole thing in play for little more than fifteen hours of abandon.

Then again, feeling alive wasn't nothing, she thought as she examined the underside of the leaves on the rubber tree for scale. The experience of George had been more complicated than sex; it had revived a yearning she'd begun to doubt. Perversely, thanks to her experiment, for the first time in years she was absolutely certain she wanted to keep Peter. Fucking George stopped her from wondering what she could have—maybe, possibly—if she ventured out into the world. Now she knew that she would not give up any part of the solid, dull, predictable life she shared with Peter for an unknowable and undoubtedly idealized freedom. Yes, the scale was spreading. Damn! It was next to impossible to get rid of. Superfamily Coccoidea. Named for their creepy resemblance to reptilian scales. After hatching, the parasites choose a spot, secret themselves beneath a waxy cover, and never move again.

Peter aimlessly wandered the apartment. He'd read the *Times* and eaten a large sandwich with potato chips and a Coke for lunch hours ago. He'd wanted a beer with the sandwich, but it wasn't a thing he allowed himself at home. Somehow day drinking was okay on vacation but not at home, even on a Saturday. Scrolling through Twitter, he was washed in the vitriolic dialogue of a world at odds on every front. He swiped up to close the app.

Leaning his head back on the sofa, he closed his eyes. Instantly, his mind populated with images of Lisbeth. Pushing the thought away, he considered Alice. She'd been vaguely inaccessible for the past year—since the girls left. But ever since the dog disappeared she'd been truly absent. It was as if he didn't exist. Her self-sufficiency was insulting, and yet it had the effect of liberating him. Maybe that was it, he thought: he was free for the first time in twenty-two years, so he'd found Lisbeth. But was he really free? No. His entanglement with Alice was integral to him. They'd grown over and through each other. Looking toward the sill with its endless greenery, he imagined two plants crammed into one pot, the roots competing for water and nutrients, slowly strangling each other. But the overwrought metaphor was off and he knew it. More accurately, he and Alice were two species grafted together, like those tacky fruit trees in the back of the *New Yorker* that bear apples and pears. Once done, the unnatural composite was permanent.

Why did he feel like a fraud? His identity as a doctor—as an analyst—took up most of his mental space while the long work days occupied most of his waking hours. He had built a reputation for himself. He was respected in his field. Beyond his practice he'd tried to be a good husband and father. Adequately providing for the three women he loved most in the world meant something, surely. Why wasn't it enough? Why did he suddenly feel reckless? Perhaps, he thought, it was that famous death instinct, the instinct toward self-destruction that drew him toward his young patient. It wasn't an attraction. It was a denial. It was Eros versus Thanatos or, as Freud would have it, the death wish versus the pleasure principle. Why wouldn't he be rooting for pleasure to win? To hell with it. Being a psychiatrist didn't make him a saint.

Alice left the room with the watering can. At it again. If it wasn't the dog, it was the fucking plants. Was there a limit to how many plants Alice would cram into the space? He liked the greenery well enough, but her preoccupation with grooming the plants irritated him. Why did she have to be so excessive? Her affections, whether for the dog or her plants or her wild theories about what he understood as the mechanics of bird movement were endearing—until they weren't. More and more often, they provoked a quiet rage in him.

As he wrestled with the breadth of his anger over the endless drama—the dog, the plants, the girls, money—he slowed his thoughts and then staunched them. He missed the girls and the dog, too. But he went on with his work. He had to. Why did he allow her to get to him? Why did her behavior threaten him? For the second time in a month he wished for an analyst of his own.

Picking up his phone to scroll down the top stories in the *Times*, Peter wondered what Alice was doing in her room. The door was now closed and their policy, although unspoken, was not to disturb each other when their doors were closed unless absolutely necessary. Even then, they'd text or even call room to room. Neither of them considered this arrangement cold—it was practical and preserved the privacy each felt in their own space. He closed the *Times* app and texted her.

Peter: *Dinner?*

Within moments the ghostly dots of her imminent response wavered on his screen.

Alice: *Dunno. Chinese? BBQ?*

Peter: *Dino?*

Alice: *Sure! Sounds good.*

Fake enthusiasm, Peter thought irritably as Alice emerged from her room. Using a dish towel to twist the cap off a beer, she sat down at the counter. The Seamless app indicated their dinner was eighteen minutes away. He sat staring at his phone, his feet on the coffee table over the face of Alden Ehrenreich on the cover of an old *Esquire*.

I've put up all those flyers. It's been over three weeks, and we haven't had so much as a text, Alice began. I wonder if we should increase the reward?

I don't know. What do all the websites say? What did that group you met with advise? he asked. Peter thought $2,000 was more than adequate, but he wasn't in the mood for a fight. He hated the idea of the Facebook group. He hated Facebook. Certainly, it had its utility in this situation, but the idea of meeting people who had identified one another on the platform seemed risky and desperate. Alice had later said the meeting was a waste of time, just as he'd predicted.

I don't know. They all seem to have offered larger rewards. But their dogs were really expensive. They're all hiring pet detectives.

Pet detectives? That's a joke, he said.

Inwardly, she writhed. Discussing the meeting felt dangerous. A wave of shame washed over her. She was afraid of blushing. Keeping her eyes down, she took a sip of her beer and opened Instagram to distract herself. Tears slid slowly down her cheeks but wiping them would have drawn Peter's attention to her—and to them. She let them go, focusing as hard as she could on a photo of the Donnes eating truffled pasta in Siena.

Peter felt a great wave of sympathy for Alice. She was silently, almost stoically weeping. He couldn't go to her. Physical touch was electrically charged. How had they gotten to this point? Worse, he'd made fun of the idea of a pet detective, and here she was just holding it together. But where the fuck was the food? Reflexively he picked up his phone to check the delivery time. He knew he should get up and hug her, but he didn't want to. At best it would be one of those stiff-bodied hugs—all self-consciousness on both sides, arms and heads having nowhere to land; at worst she'd cringe as if he were about to strike her. The food looked to be just minutes out.

I'm sorry, Alice. Think of it this way: Whoever has her probably loves her. They would return her if they didn't. She'll be fine.

He knew this was an inadequate response, at once cold and false. Just then, the buzzer sounded. Saved by the pork.

By the time he was back in the kitchen with the food, she'd wiped her face and appeared calmer. Hating himself for it, he was pleased she'd pulled herself together. He was hungry. They settled in the den, flicked through the apps and several saved shows on their TiVo only to predictably settle on a recording of Friday's *Rachel Maddow*.

Between ribs, Alice ate forkfuls of slaw wet with hot sauce while Peter consumed two squares of cornbread cut in half with cold butter in between. Alice watched and listened to him chew, vaguely repulsed by his overindulgence in the cornbread-butter sandwiches. The noise of his tongue in the mash of cornbread was spoiling her appetite. She felt for the remote in the cushions behind her. Peter looked at her questioningly, a yellow crumb on his lip making him look ridiculous.

I can't hear a thing, she said.

Oh. Seems pretty loud. Whatever.

The evasive little gadget in hand, she turned up the volume a few clicks. She could still hear him chewing.

Licking their fingers and drinking beer, they were finished eating even before Maddow's overwrought buildup had yielded to the big reveal. Peter cleared the plates and silverware while Alice gathered up the wadded barbecue sauce–stained paper towels and empty clamshells. Before dumping them in the garbage, she stared at the messy pile of gnawed bones, so stripped of all meat they appeared to have been sucked clean. What vicious carnivores they were. The bones had belonged to more than one live pig, and they'd mixed the animals' carcasses together without thinking. Mixing the bones of the dead was as taboo as cannibalism.

Sitting on the sofa alone, all Alice could think about was Maebelle's absence. The indelible image of her earnest, deeply attentive face peering up at them as they consumed a meal in front of the TV looped through her mind. She knew she wouldn't be given any of the pork bones but the possibility that a crumb of cornbread or shred of meat would fall to the floor seemed to satisfy her as she held her vigilant watch.

If she could have Alice in sight at all times—or one of the girls if they were home—she was fulfilled. In their absence, Alice suspected the world was a living hell to her. Waiting, in this state with nothing right in her mind, she exemplified the condition of loneliness, a state in which the world was wrong and could be made right only by the addition of a single human being. What a vulnerable way to be. Alice hated the thought. It wasn't often that she was aware of how lonely she was, but now she recognized how Maebelle's company confused her isolation, tricking her mind into thinking she was less alone than she was. She yearned for sleep but she had hours to go before she'd be tired. If only she drank whiskey. That would have put her out.

Friday–Sunday, July 6–8, July 4 Observed

Purchasing a house and a beach view on the Cape in 1978 didn't take a million—never mind two or three. Excess assets, thanks to a small inheritance from Anna's father, mixed with real estate luck were in the air when Anna and Will Darling caught sight of the modern, light-blue clapboard at 222 Nauset Light Beach Road. A mere forty-eight days passed between their first sighting and the fraught moment of entering what they suddenly owned but didn't know. At least you could test-drive a car before you bought it. To overnight in a house before committing to what was for many—though not the Darlings—the biggest purchase of your life seemed reasonable. In the end it didn't matter. The house wasn't the point. It sat perched on the bluff in full command of the Cape Cod National Seashore. They'd paid for the best view in Barnstable County. You didn't even need to step inside the house to know that.

Exotic decoration of the wide deck overlooking the ocean included candles, tree-worthy planters, mirrors, and masses of colorful, embroidered pillows to cushion the ancient wicker furniture Anna had inherited from her father. Its scale and intricacy was reminiscent of the Raffles Hotel circa 1920. Shipped back from Singapore in the 1960s, the furniture carried an air of privilege, reminding Alice of sterling silver trays, Singapore Slings, and houseboys in livery. These associations adhered to the scooped lounges and oversize chairs despite New England's air of chilly Puritan austerity.

When the deck cascaded down the bank into the ocean, Alice visualized the weathered boards as a flotilla heaving with the North Atlantic swells, a bobbing way station for migrating birds. The reality was that the deck had been smashed as the sand eroded fifty feet beneath it, sending the flimsy structure over the cliff as a mess of splintered boards that would be further crushed by pounding waves.

Since the deck's demise five years before, the furniture had been placed in a sorry cluster around the side of the house where it gathered spiders and bird shit, the wanton air of Rajasthani hippie abandon lost to the Atlantic with the wood that had supported it. The ocean was closing in fast. When they'd arrived two months ago, the Darlings had found that a massive winter storm had taken out several more precious feet of their shoreline. The edge of the septic tank and the concrete foundation were now visible from the beach below. It was as if the house had sustained a compound fracture, its very bones protruding from the soil.

Bing's Movers were making a killing moving houses to the back of property lines up and down the Cape's shoreline. It wasn't cheap, but the properties were worth between two and three million—or would have been if they weren't part of an ongoing environmental calamity. As the one- or two-acre-deep lots shrank at the rate of roughly six inches per year, the back of each parcel slowly became its front, once-square lots elongating into narrow claims on the ocean view that would, eventually, be erased entirely. The molecular politics of shear: land turned to air by tidal surges performing a cruel, unnecessary repossession.

The Darlings' summer house was falling into the sea, and everything that could be done to save it had been done. Unmoored from the earth ten years earlier, it had been lifted and set back down at the back of the property line. There was nowhere else to go. Even though it was not yet gone, Alice was prematurely nostalgic for the quaint, useless kitchen, where for decades they'd prepared blueberry pancakes, lobster rolls, slaw and steamers with sunburnt children underfoot, anxious to get to the beach with their buckets and towels. She'd miss the slanted floors and doors that didn't close, the smell of musty books overlain with briny moisture, but most of all she'd miss the prodigal view where they'd sat with cocktails and wine to mark the dying day, the children playing together elsewhere as the adults grew progressively louder and more boisterous with drink. It was the unobstructed purity of communion with the seamless lines of sky, dune, and water that gave the house its charm. The house's fate sickened Alice.

She, Peter, and the girls had spent the Fourth of July there for the past fifteen years; for the past five they'd left feeling sad, saying goodbye as if to an elderly relative, knowing it might be the last sight of them before they go to the grave. One properly organized nor'easter, with the devastating wind, snow, and rain of a macroscale extratropical cyclone, would eliminate the house from the bluff.

Alice's attachment to the structure went beyond their July visits there as a family. Six years ago she'd worked there for the month of June on a paper for *Quanta* magazine, *Flight by Sight: Pixilated Hyper-Uniformity, Sturnus vulgaris, and Murmurations as Expressions of Hydrodynamic Chaos.* The Darlings' daughter was marrying in London and they were making a European tour of it. For the first time since 1978 they would not be there in June. Knowing her friend was finishing a paper having to do with something or other about birds in flight, Anna practically begged Alice to use the house. There could be no more ideal setting for her work than the terminally doomed structure, with its salt air carrying the raucous sound of the gulls that flew in cocky gangs over the beach, riding the currents of air at eye level just to show off. Being on the same plane with birds was a sort of professional ideal for Alice—no matter they were gulls, not starlings.

When it came to the dangerous pleasures of ocean swimming, Peter was like a child, content to pass hours dipping and diving, splashing and rolling about in the light-gravity medium. Seeing him in the water reminded Alice of the hours he'd passed playing with the girls in every hotel pool they'd ever had access to, no matter how puny, cold, or fetid with chlorine.

On Friday morning she and Peter made their way down the steep, perilous stairway to the beach for the first time that summer. Tucking their oversize towels together on the warm sand, they ventured slowly into the waves, giggling like children as the chilly water reached the sensitive skin of their bellies. It was their first Fourth of July weekend without the girls. If it were possible after twenty-two years of life together, Alice experienced a mild self-consciousness entering the water with Peter as a couple—or perhaps it was simply her awareness of wanting to make it a success and knowing, in the absence of the girls, it was now up to her. The imperative to make it fun forced Alice to remain in much longer than she normally would have. Surprised by how invigorated she felt, she reveled in the hardy strength of her body in the bracing water as she dove hard under the waves only to emerge breathless on the other side, ready to duck again as the next wave broke. New York felt distant and small.

Peter and Alice swam in the waves that day for more than an hour. In the water they were a team, reliant on the other's presence as each periodically made sure the other was still afloat. Their alliance against the abstract dangers of sharks, rogue waves, and currents gave the swim a surprising intimacy.

Heading for shore at last, they lingered, captivated by the sight of a herd of seals watching them, the animals' gentle faces peering curiously toward them over the swells as they tracked the humans in the midst. From a distance, the seals' big black eyes and noses set off by floppy whiskers gave them a canine quality. Neither of them spoke of it.

Anna had worked all morning while her guests swam, her lush dark curls spilling over the pages of the financial statements she expertly made sense of. She always seemed to be working, meeting the ever-expanding demands of her job as CFO of Woman-2-Woman, the internet-based lingerie company she'd founded with her friend Dahlia. They both designed the functional but slinky silk negligees, bras, and nighties that accommodated the bodies of model size 00 to the buxom plus-sizers in need of a 22. They'd begun the company as an antidote to their daughters' infatuation with the sexually predatory vibe of Victoria's Secret.

Anna was a surprising combination; a numbers girl who could also sew, draw, knit, and cook. Alice considered her talents as she scraped the sunken bits of tender potato and chewy clam from the bottom of the chowder bowl Anna had placed in front of her. Will opened a beer—it was a holiday weekend, after all—and Peter joined him. The men, engaged in a discussion of Will's latest case, didn't seem to have much interest in talking to the women. This suited Alice nicely. Will was such a bore with his lawyer talk. So she sipped iced tea and queried Anna about the risks of taking on venture capital. Anna wasn't sure it was time to expand their business into stand-alone brick-and-mortar stores. It was easy for Alice to encourage her to think big, her displaced desire for her friend's financial success no more than an abstraction to her.

As they dispersed after lunch, Alice felt a sadness settle over her as she relaxed into the fatigue of the long swim. She missed Maebelle. She'd been her companion for that long stretch alone there all those years ago—walking with her on the beach, running to and fro on the shore, barking as Alice swam, and sleeping, as always, under the covers while she listened to the sound of the wind rattling the walls of the old house. Remembering what they referred to as *the Maebelle incident* that year, Alice experienced a flash of the humiliation she had briefly felt at the time.

Returning from the grocery store one day, she'd found a note slipped under the front door. It read:

To the resident(s)
222 Nauset Light Beach Road
Eastham, MA

It has been peaceful and quiet here for many years until you arrived with your noisy, barking dog.

For the past week, you have allowed your dog the freedom to roam the property of other residents. We have been awakened at 6 AM several mornings by your dog barking on our property.

We have also observed the animal running loose and defecating on our properties at various times throughout the day.

This rude practice needs to be stopped immediately so that further action need not be taken.

Concerned Residents of
Nauset Light Beach Road

cc: Eastham Police Department

Shocked, she'd read the letter again. Her humiliation then burned to outrage only to settle submissively into amusement. The shift to the royal *we* in the second paragraph particularly galled her when she knew it was one nasty neighbor, a woman living alone to the south, who'd written the letter. The fussy language and oddly declarative paragraphs topped off by the threat of *further action* were preposterous—as was the cc to the police. Since when, in the country, did dogs not wander freely to shit wherever they happened to sniff and squat? The land-scape was a wild mix of *Rosa rugosa*, potted plants, and scrubby undergrowth. There wasn't a single lawn to soil because noth-ing more demanding than stray tufts of beach grass grew on the bluff. It was a reclaimed sand dune, as was dramatically illustrated by the fate of the Darlings' house.

Alice had kept Maebelle on a tight rein after that while trying to laugh at the bitter, bored old woman who lacked the courage or decency to sign her name, much less simply knock on her door and make a polite request. The memory of the incident felt painful but also, still, a little funny. Would that Mae-belle were there to elicit the wrath of the neighborhood witch.

Saturday night the four of them went out to eat at the local clam shack—something of a misnomer for a place that sold $30 buckets of fried clams, fried scallop sandwiches with aioli, and $25 lobster rolls, but going there was a ritual they weren't about to change when soon enough it would all be over. Alice chewed the whole-belly clams, the hot guts mushy and rich as organ meat with the tiniest hint of grit to remind her of the sand flat where they'd been dug earlier that day.

That evening, Alice stared at the sunset over the Atlantic, the strips of pink and orange glowing as the day submitted to night, the sky splendid from the royal perspective of the bluff. She was determined to observe the sunset—not to capture it for eternity with a picture and certainly not lob it on to Instagram supported by a wry caption.

There was nothing surprising about sharing a bed with Peter. They'd shared one for more than twenty years before taking to their own. The familiarity of his movement, the way he balled the sheet in his fist and curled into a fetal position, had long since ceased to surprise her, the incongruity of the big man in such an infant pose having gained the invisibility of the familiar. When she woke at 3 AM to his guttural, snorting breathing Alice didn't bother to nudge him. It was the wine, her throbbing head, and thirst that had woken her, not his usual nighttime theatrics.

Opening her eyes again hours later, Alice smelled breakfast. She'd finally fallen asleep, covering her head with the pillow to muffle Peter's snores. Imperfectly rested, she got up. The meaty, smoky smell of bacon mixed with the mint toothpaste foaming in her mouth as she stood staring at her reflection left her vaguely nauseated. Dabbing cover-up over the dark circles under her eyes, she smeared on a gloss of lip color and settled with what she saw staring back at her. The summer tan she'd cemented in place in the past two days had done much to improve the appearance of her skin. Surely, she'd end up looking like those women who spent too much time in the sun, their faces craggy and leathery next to their better-kept, more prudent sisters whose obsession with shade and sunscreen ensured their skin stayed pure, uncreased, and pale as a geisha's. It wasn't in her nature to be so careful. She couldn't resist the heat of the sun on her face and the faux-healthy appearance of a tan.

As she entered the kitchen, Will was working the stove, tending a big sauté pan of scrambled eggs to which he'd added cream cheese and leftover diced shishito peppers. On the table he'd set out the remainder of the Zabar's smoked salmon they'd arrived with along with bialys, bagels, sliced onion, capers, and tomato. On a pretty pink floral plate Anna had stacked pecan sticky buns from their favorite bakery in Provincetown. Will poured Alice a cup of coffee.

Where the man?

Where do you think? I'm sure you'll hear him if you listen.

Ha! He does have an impressive snore. I almost envy it. How did you sleep? Or do you sleep?

Well, twenty-two years later I'm not sure what to tell you. We manage. And you, did you sleep? Those buns look decadent. I think you're trying to make me fat.

I try.

Indeed he does, chimed in Anna as she entered from the driveway, the bulky plastic-swathed tube of the Sunday *New York Times* in hand. She gave Alice an affectionate kiss, adding, Good morning! You slept! It's already nine.

It can't be. Really? Alice's phone had died playing BBC to her insomnia. She had no idea what time it was. I hope we didn't keep breakfast waiting.

No, no. I'm teasing. We slept in, too.

After all the damage we did . . .

Alice poured milk into her coffee. It was good and hot, just the way she liked it. All she needed now was one of those sweet buns and a cigarette. She wondered if she could manage it. Like any addict, she was always scheming how to get the next fix. Could she step outside on the pretense of getting something out of the car or pretend she wanted to take a quick walk on the beach? Hardly. Not with the eggs almost ready and the bacon in the warming oven. It would have to wait. She needed to rouse Peter and get on the road. The notorious Bourne Bridge bottleneck awaited.

Finally settled at table, with Peter looking groggy and hungover to her left, Alice sipped freshly squeezed grapefruit juice from an ancient, fragile tumbler, the pale pink bittersweet fruit juice showing through the cut glass. Napkins on laps, coffee in hand, the four of them passed plates, onions, tomato, butter, salt, and pepper.

Momentarily frozen by her own thoughts, Alice reddened. Happily for her, nobody at the table noticed as they argued over the merits of Wianno versus Onset versus Wellfleet and whether or not you could taste the difference between a farm-raised and a wild oyster. Rather than chiming in with the definitive, scientific answer to the silly question they were discussing, Alice indulged her reverie.

Breakfast. No, room service. But first she'd woken that day to the clattering of George opening the blinds that had kept the sky glow of the city from filtering into the room—they were so high up there was nothing more than ambient light, sky, and the occasional bird or helicopter on the other side of the massive windowpane. Turning at the sound of her *Good morning*, George had approached the bed silently while holding eye contact. He'd wrapped a towel around his waist but his broad, smooth chest and shapely shoulders were on lovely display. Men were generally not pretty creatures with all their lumps, hair, and thickness; he was exceptional. Reaching the bed he dropped the towel, placed his hands and knees on the bed and inched toward her, crawling like a big cat. Just before she thought he was going to kiss her as she sat staring, smiling in embarrassment at his playful, silent movement toward her, he abruptly pulled the covers down, exposing her nakedness. Alice had protested, briefly horrified at the prospect of her aging flesh on display beneath the harsh morning rays streaming through the east-facing window. But before she could, he had his mouth on her belly button while gently pulling one leg toward him. Climbing over it, he compressed himself at the end of the bed while pushing her legs apart. Her sex, suddenly very much awake, became the center of her consciousness as the energy around it activated. Reaching both of his big hands beneath her hips, he shoved her body farther up the bed, allowing himself room to work before disappearing. Expertly parting her labia with his tongue, he then began licking the length of her from anus to clit. Starting so slowly it was a tease, he gradually increased his speed, the sensation each time his tongue reached her clit causing an agonizing desire for him to focus on it and only it. Close to begging him to finish her, he suddenly began working on her right there—his dexterity bringing her off to stupendous effect. She'd tried to pull him up, breathing hard, close to coming—part of her wanted to extend the orgasm, save it. She'd also badly wanted him in her—that stiff prick she could feel against her knee, she wanted it hard in her. But he'd finished her off just as he pleased, at his own pace, only then sliding up, kissing her from the eyes to the nose to the mouth. Tasting herself just as he pushed into her, she wasn't sure at that moment how she'd be able to give the man up. With his strong arms over her, the rhythm of his movements effortless yet decisive—even forceful—she gripped the headboard and reveled in the novelty of submission, conscious of the desire to be further dominated and humiliated, one she hadn't known—

Alice. Oh, Alice . . . Peter called, trying to get her attention, as if from a great distance. Everyone at the table was looking at her, waiting for her to snap out of her reverie. Could you please pass the cream cheese? Reaching to her side, she dreamily lifted the earthy porcelain crock and handed it to him.

I want to be where Alice was, said Anna slyly.

Yeah, me too. To hell with breakfast, added Will.

Peter looked at her as he covered a sesame bagel with an inch of cream cheese.

Me three, he said grimly.

Tuesday, July 17

He hadn't meant to do it. Before Lisbeth left after her noon appointment she'd been telling him about another dream, this time even more explicit. The two of them were in bed together. It had been lush despite the white sheets and hard brightness—daylight indoors. She described it as if the bed they shared was in a field on a cloudless day in summer. They were entwined in each other's limbs, the safety and comfort of the experience taking precedence over the sexual. With a brief wave of humiliation he'd felt his excitement—how could he not? There she sat in her tiny skirt, the tan perfection of thighs, knees, calves, and ankles falling to the floor where they met strappy red patent flats. The blue top she wore was sheer enough to see the outline of her dark nipples—Peter thought he could even discern the texture of areola, but maybe it was just the fabric. She didn't need really to wear a bra—and she hadn't.

And then time had been up and what to do with himself? He didn't know any other way to disperse the tension of his desire—which was not a physical tension but a mental preoccupation that made him badly want the orgasm that he knew would

come on, fast and thrilling, the moment he unzipped. Standing
to lock the door—a thing he never did during the day—he lay
on his unused green analyst's couch. At least it was good for
something, he thought ruefully as he freed his fully erect penis.
The eroticism of thinking of the girl while coming in the room
where her particular scent still lingered had him moving toward
the finish far too quickly. Slowing his hand, he thought of Alice—
nothing slowed him down more than the memory of sex with
her, the reluctance of her participation in the act making it almost
impossible for him to come at all. Impotence had never been a
problem—until it had become one with Alice. It had everything
to do with her inability to measure up to the lusty images he'd
become so familiar with, the screen babes who talked him along
in their scant lingerie, the Asian girls practically squeaking with
pleasure. Turning his head toward the chair where Lisbeth sat
each session, he returned to her, remembering the long black
hair and imagining the feel of her small, tight breasts and what
he imagined was her pristine, beardless cunt. He visualized her
kneeling to the side of the analyst's couch with his cock in her
big, gorgeous mouth.

She loved to give head. She'd actually said that. Some
women did. He believed her when she said it—even if she might
have said it to provoke him. The idea that she was doing her
best to seduce him wasn't in question, nor was how completely
irrelevant that effort was to his behavior. Unable to hold back with
the visual of her long hair falling across his belly, his hand on the
back of her head, guiding her mouth, he came in one spectacular
jolt, barely preventing his cum from landing on the couch. All
he could be thankful for as he stood, pulling his pants straight
and tightening his belt, was that his next patient was George.

It was just his second session and they'd covered only the barest preliminaries, but the elegant doctor in his fifties was a man he suspected, from the careful grooming and perfect manners, must do very nicely with women. If he'd known what Peter had just done, he might have understood; he was a doctor, after all. Perhaps he'd done the same himself after seeing a particularly attractive patient? Although Peter hadn't yet grasped the nature of George's practice, he would surely appreciate Lisbeth himself. He should take care they didn't mingle in the waiting room. One never knew with their types: gorgeous, both of them, and so prime for sexual adventure. There was no knowing what might come of it.

I'm not here to complain about my wife, he began, settling in the chair. She's perfect—a saint, really. I'm a lucky man. But something's wrong. I've been unfaithful—quite a cad, really. More than once. Hmmm. Five times? It doesn't really matter. You must think I'm a pig.

Peter looked at him. He would have preferred his patient to continue. The man seemed to know the game well enough to force Peter to speak by outpacing his silence. *Speaking of pigs*, he wanted to say, *you have no idea*. Instead, he relented with a neutral pushback: What I think isn't really important.

The titillating confession that followed beat the hell out of listening to the repetitive admissions of his depressed and eating disordered patients.

I wouldn't be here except that it just recently started bothering me. I cheated on my wife for the first time ten years ago. That's not important. The thing is, I can't seem to get the latest one out of my head. There was something about it that stuck with me—it wasn't the sex. We talked for hours and hours first. Theresa, my wife, was out of town, but I took her to a hotel anyway—it feels kinder not to cheat on your wife in the marital bed, no?

Keeping his silence, Peter wondered if his patient was looking for confirmation of his decency, or had he assumed he had cheated on his wife as well? Did he appear as guilty as he felt? Was there a scent of something coming off him that gave it away?

She was very attractive, don't get me wrong. And the sex. Well, the sex was as good as sex with someone you don't know very well is—steamier than it can possibly be with someone you've been sharing a bed with for two decades. It's nobody's fault— Theresa's amazing. And beautiful. But sex between us is . . . I don't need to go into the details of the sex with you, Dr. Nutting. And I'd like to stay focused. I really don't have time for therapy. Actually, I really can't believe I'm here. It's crazy. I'm hoping, as I said the other day, I'm hoping to have a few sessions to sort this out and be on my way. In truth, I haven't even told my wife.

You haven't told your wife what, exactly?

Oh, sorry. I haven't told my wife about coming here.

I see. Any idea why it's important for you to keep it secret? Peter realized what a stupid question it was the moment he'd said it. The guy would have to make up a reason or tell her he'd been cheating on her and wanted to figure out why. Stupid. It was easy to omit. Peter knew this as well as the best of them.

I try not to lie to my wife. Which is why I'm here. Not telling her about my dalliances over the years is starting to get to me. I mean, maybe that's why the last one has been so distracting. I think it was the conversation. She was in my field, so we had a lot to talk about. You know how it is when you talk to someone and they get everything you say and ask the right questions. I'm sure you must feel that way with your fellow therapists. It's a language. You read the same journals, know the same people, suffer the same quandaries, share social media interests. My wife never asked, of course. Why would she? But I haven't offered, and the sin of omission is certainly on me.

I'm hearing you say your relationship with your wife isn't physically satisfying. You're expressing some sense of guilt about your infidelity. What I'm not sure about is whether you're here because you want to stop or because you want permission to continue.

Hmmm. Permission. What would that look like? A paper slip from the good doctor in inscrutable doctor cursive that says George may be excused today—no, tonight!—from his marital obligations due to acute moral failure.

Peter smiled.

You consider it a moral failing? It clearly weighs on your conscience. I often wonder when a patient tells me they're doing something they regret, and repeating the action, which they again regret, what the guilt is doing for them. Peter was thinking of his bulimic patients but the magic of holding on to secrets was another compelling motive for acting out. Do you feel a need to berate yourself? Is there something compelling about being bad in this way, beyond the pleasures of the sex and conversation?

Perhaps. I've been dutiful. I've worked hard all my life. I married a woman with money—but I loved her. I'm not suggesting I married her for the money . . .

He protested too much, thought Peter. He had married for the money—at least it had been a more significant factor than he liked to admit to himself. And he'd just used the past tense of *love*. Peter thought about Alice. What it would be to have a wife with money. What it would be to afford a house in the country, a garden to give Alice an outlet for her insatiable plant lust, a spacious house where the girls could bring their college friends for Thanksgiving, a wood-fired grill. Peter brought himself back to focus. George was still talking money.

. . . she so happens to have a great deal of it. Maybe for me to step outside the lines is a way of insisting she doesn't own me. Hmmm. That feels too simple, but maybe there's something there. When I was with this most recent woman—let's call her five for the sake of it. Or, he said, looking up at Peter with a wicked twinkle, we could go with a color scheme: Mrs. Pink, Mrs. White, Mrs. Orange. You know? *Reservoir Dogs* style.

Withholding her name feels important? Somehow honorable? he asked. Peter wasn't sure what to do with the violence at the core of the film George had referenced, so he let it slide. Why were his patients always referring to films he hadn't seen or could hardly remember?

I guess so. It seems wrong to throw the names around—not that saying them here would matter. I guess I owe them some discretion just as I owe my wife the courtesy not to fuck them in our bed. Then again, it's all very convenient for me, these little courtesies. I didn't bring the last one home because, although my wife was away, the maid would have noticed the sheets and the doorman would see her come and go in the morning. It's a bitch to cheat on your wife with a doorman. He laughed, as if Peter knew exactly what a bitch it was to cheat on your wife with a doorman. But he didn't. Not only because he didn't have a doorman but also because he hadn't ever cheated on Alice. He felt like a Boy Scout next to George. And, of course, he had a point. It would be hell. Thank god there wasn't any shortage of hotels in Manhattan. And how much sexier that would be anyway. Peter had a flash of taking Lisbeth to a hotel, watching her emerge nude from the immaculate bathroom, her slim body against the stunning skyline of the city—stopping himself, he returned to the session by restating what George had just said. It was the oldest, sorriest shrink trick in the book.

You seem to be acknowledging a more utilitarian side to what you initially presented as a courtesy to your wife.

You're saying I'm a devious bastard? George playfully asked, showing his blindingly white teeth.

Not at all. I'm simply trying to scrape away at the defenses. I'm trying to get us to the bottom of what you want and why.

What I want and why, George repeated.

I guess two can play that game, Peter thought.

What I want is number five. Why? Because she was just so ethereal and complicated. I didn't feel I could have her even if I wanted her—more than the once, I mean. I met her because she burst into tears. It just happened. We were making small talk, and then she was crying. I love it when women cry—sorry, that sounded terrible. I'm not a sadist. I love the vulnerability a woman shows when she cries, not that she's in distress. It was so adorable. Her nose went red and the rims of her eyes swelled in the classic tear response.

A woman crying makes many men uncomfortable. You find it attractive. Any thoughts about that?

Hmm, was all he said. He paused, thinking. Peter gave him time, inviting a weighty silence to fill the tiny room to the point of discomfort. Finally, George spoke.

It's interesting. I never really thought about it, but my mother was a crier. I was always able to comfort her. I'd come home from school to find her alone in the house, her swollen eyes and red nose a giveaway no matter what she'd done to conceal the evidence. Every day after I got off the bus I'd sit in the kitchen watching her make me a sandwich. It was always bologna on white with mustard and mayo. Not much of a sandwich, really, by today's standards. But it was my favorite. I still love that sandwich. Theresa thinks it's repulsive. I buy Oscar Mayer bologna, and she throws it out. What is it about women cleaning out the refrigerator? Anyway, so my beautiful mom would sit down at the kitchen table with me, a cup of black coffee and a Winston Light, and we'd talk. She was such a generous conversationalist. She'd take in the smallest details of my day, behaving as though school cafeteria seating arrangements, the class ranking on the spelling test, and boys' locker room jokes were fascinating. So I'd tell her more, and she'd ask questions. She knew everyone I was talking about because I'd been going to school with them all since kindergarten. We had our own little soap opera going. And then she'd add what she knew about the parents—nothing too indiscreet. Just that so-and-so's dad had lost his job, or someone's parents were getting divorced, or someone was straying. It took me the longest time to figure out what that meant. She'd been saying it to me all my life: Mrs. Morrison is straying. Mitch's dad strayed. All I could think of was a cat. Cats stray—they go out and then they wander—sometimes they don't come back.

Then there was the band—the Stray Cats. Remember the hit "(She's) Sexy + 17"? So if Mrs. Morrison was straying, I could hardly blame her. Who didn't like to get out a bit? In fact, I wondered why my mother didn't stray—everyone else seemed to be doing it. It wasn't until senior year in high school that I finally figured out what she meant. But I made the connection because I had just seen my father with another woman in town. I was coming home on the bus from a debate club meeting at another school and right there, coming out of the steak house on Elm Street in Caldwell, the next town over, was my dad with a woman who was not my mom. I knew right then that they were fucking each other. I was still a virgin, but I'd had a taste by then of how to take charge of a girl you wanted. Suddenly I knew. Not only was my dad sleeping with that woman but he'd also been behaving as though he was the caretaker and boss of the woman I'd grown up with my whole life. I guess I learned the behavior from him. It's almost a set of moves. Really, it's all about the hands. Touching the shoulder. Moving a strand of hair out of a woman's face. Plucking a bit of lint from her clothing. Hand on the back. Simple intimacies. It was as though I absorbed them or inherited them, as if there is a gene for touching. Anyway, when my mother said later that week that my father was straying again, I put it all together. What a little idiot I was. I suppose I knew but didn't want to—didn't want to *know* it. I don't think that's why my mother cried all the time. I think she was just a brilliant woman trapped. She'd gotten pregnant while she was working at a bank straight out of college. It wasn't a great job but, knowing Mom, if she'd stayed she would have been the bank president before she was thirty. Instead she had me, and then I suppose she got depressed. My father was a lawyer—a company lawyer. Procter and Gamble. He traveled a lot, leaving me and Mom to play board games and watch movies. She was terrific.

George's voice had tightened over the course of the narrative.

Is your mother still alive?

Peter could tell from the way his voice closed down that she wasn't, but this was where they'd ended up, and it was a good, solid point of departure as it turned out. What could be more relevant to the man's complaint than his dead mother who reminded him of number five, his cheating father, and his role as savior? He loved it when a patient unloaded such a rich trove early on. What he wouldn't give for such details and insight in half his other patients.

She died five years ago. Ovarian cancer. I had her at Sloan Kettering but there was nothing for it. As you know, you see that in your biopsy results, and it's like seeing death right there, writ large.

I'm sorry.

That's the thing about number five. She did remind me of my mother. Not that I want to sleep with my mother any more than the next guy—which is really not at all, right? What crap Freud spewed. But the unconscious. Now that's a hell of a thing to invent. But I do long for her company. I miss her presence, her humor, how she listened to me, how proud she was that I became a rich doctor. So this woman, this latest woman, there was also something girlish about her, like the way I remember my mother sitting at the table, weepy. She even smoked. Who smokes anymore? But so damaged, so sad. When she cried I had an immediate impulse to rescue her, and then after we talked I was so attracted to her. Not like the other women—one through four since we're going with numbers not colors. They were just fucks. Not that there's anything wrong with that.

Peter considered George's preoccupation with these women's anonymity and the game he was playing in numbering them. Why were they important as individual numbers or colors? What was significant about the color scheme that he'd ultimately discarded? Were the women interchangeable, or did George simply want to depersonalize them, to shift the intimacy away by denying them their individuality? Most patients just stuck with the real name.

No, five was just so raw and present. Having sex with her at the Mandarin reminded me of college. The girls were sometimes not all that experienced. Don't get me wrong. She wasn't inexperienced. She's married and has kids in college— that much I know. It was more her hesitance—we didn't take it slowly, but we were careful with each other and curious. Tender the way you aren't with someone you've fucked a hundred times. I love that moment of passion, that kind of crazy hunger when you want a woman so much kissing isn't quite enough— you almost want to bite them. I started down five's pants in the elevator—couldn't stop myself. But she was game—very. The first time I cheated on my wife I met this absolutely fabulous twentysomething doctor at an infectious disease conference in Orlando. She pursued me. There's no question in my mind about that. I would not have presumed to seduce her—actually it hadn't even occurred to me to cheat on my wife. But what an incredible specimen. She did things I never knew women liked to do. Anal. What woman actually asks for anal? Not in my generation—well, our generation. No way. I've never even done it with my wife in twenty years. You?

Peter wasn't about to answer. He was a shade ashamed that he had not fucked Alice in the ass. But George had instinctively asked him as if he were chatting with a friend—not unburdening himself in a shrink's office. The question had to be contended with.

Is it important for you to know about my sexual habits?

How dainty he sounded. Sexual habits. He even disgusted himself with his shrink talk. But what else was he going to say? Always deflect the question back to the patient. Peter knew on some level the question was merely a conversational tic. But it didn't matter. He had to throw it back at George. It mattered if he mistook Peter for a friend. It mattered if he needed Peter to approve of his sexual practices. It mattered if George wanted to visualize Peter fucking his wife up the ass.

Sorry! Shit. I forgot where I was for a moment. No, no, don't tell me. You're so easy to talk to. I know it's against the rules. Back to the books, doc. Anyway. Within two hours of meeting this woman, we're in her suite at the Marriott, she's naked, lube and vibrator at the ready, and she's taking it for granted that none of it's a big deal. I must say I felt a little old. Not for long. Jesus. It's the holy frontier. You know, we belong to the wrong generation. These women. They're lusty and hungry and they do not fuck around—well, they do, actually.

If Peter were a better man—and a better psychiatrist—he would not have experienced a wave of envy at this moment. But he did. He wanted desperately to take Lisbeth from behind, position her over the high end of the couch where he'd be level with her ass and have her that way—or any way. Stirring, he focused on George. What had George just said? His patient had removed himself from the realm of sadness and loss that had choked him up when discussing his mother. He'd made this leap, effectively cutting himself off from the emotions elicited by his memories of her, by bringing up the lusty, bad-boy fun of anal sex with a woman young enough to be his daughter. How familiar. Here he was, lusting after a woman the same age as most of George's conquests. You couldn't fight biology. That was what Peter told himself; his biological self was driven to reproduce and the most viable womb was that of a young woman. It wasn't nice. But it was the truth. Peter glanced at the clock. Saved by the bell. It always came through for him.

Time's up for today I'm afraid. I'll see you next week.

Right. Thank you. See you then.

And with that George picked up what was a very handsome, cognac leather Le Feuillet briefcase and slipped out the door. As Peter sat down to make a few notes on the session, he thought about George. What manhood. A rich doctor with a taste for the sartorial that he pulled off as though he were born to be measured and draped in the finest Italian, British, and Irish fabric. In fact, Peter was more right than he knew; it was only Dormeuil, Loro Piana, and Philip Treacy for George. But he wasn't born to it; he'd married all that class having grown up in a Podunk Pennsylvania town. Peter dressed respectably enough for work—neat khakis, shirts, and sweaters. Natural fabrics but not infrequently made in China. Not that he noticed. He wasn't embarrassed about his clothes, but he was aware of them enough to question how tasteful they were or if this George might have seen them as shoddy. He needed to upgrade his clothes—and teeth. The teeth on that man. Should he have his whitened?

Monday, July 23

Therapy, as you may recall, Peter, was once famously described as an unnatural deconstruction of desire, Dr. March began.

As Peter's supervising analyst during his years at Columbia Center for Psychoanalytic Training and Research, Dr. March's nearly bald head contained more than a brilliant mind; it contained Peter's strengths and weaknesses as an analyst. He communicated with a firm restraint that seemed at odds with his slight stoop, wire-rimmed glasses, and fringe of close-cropped white hair. Peter had arrived in his office after his last session. A fond reunion was followed by a twenty-minute explanation of where his treatment of Lisbeth stood, her condition, and most importantly his own countertransference. Coming to the end of his story, Peter realized how odd it was to be sitting in the patient's chair. It had been so long, and it felt good even if his visit wasn't really a session. It was a conversation between colleagues. In his present crisis, Peter craved his mentor's advice and yearned for his approval as never before.

As you well know, Dr. March continued, this deconstruction of desire isn't the deconstruction of your desire—it's the patient's desire. You're not a good, neutral object when you're infatuated with your patient. If you aren't doing active damage, you're at the very least her accomplice in playing out a predetermined relational erotic paradigm. You're supporting and in fact reinforcing her neurosis by reacting to her in the way you do. That's not therapy—that's malpractice.

I've strictly limited my behavior to fantasy, but the intensity is so much greater than anything I've experienced in reaction to a patient before. It's as if I woke up on the lip of a cornice just as an avalanche began, and all I can do is ski like hell while knowing that in the end I'll be buried.

That's a fine thought, and the cornice offers a surprisingly appropriate metaphor. A cornice is the condition of snow poised at the moment of transition between order and disorder. Once the snow begins to move down the mountain it becomes an enclosed system with its own self-governing laws. The metaphor suggests you feel you've *been placed* in a position, not placed yourself there, on the brink of chaos. A position, I might add, that is already out of your control. I'd suggest this is somewhat wishful thinking on your part.

The metaphor does suggest a sense of imminent catastrophe, Peter admitted. He'd have preferred his friend to be less aggressive, but this was, after all, what he'd come for. A straightening out.

Perhaps you relish the disastrous consequences you may bring on yourself as a result of your failure to manage your sexual impulses.

I have a repressed wish to destroy my practice and my marriage? You're saying this patient is simply the means to an end. She could be anyone?

Possibly. But she's not anyone. She's your patient and you have an ethical and legal duty to her. That you have private means for satisfying yourself is beside the point. You're mistaken if you think you have such exquisite control of your subconscious that you can quarantine your fantasies. That's an impossibility, as we both know. You say she's been seductive. All the more reason she needs to become a new sort of object in her interpersonal relationships, to gain a self-image that's not dependent on her primitive infantile sexual impulses. And yet, you're encouraging her to reap the rewards of maintaining a dysfunctional, self-sabotaging behavior. Honestly, how special is she to you?

I don't know. I'm not thinking of running away to Zihuatanejo with her, if that's what you're asking. He said it with an attempt at levity, then added more seriously, But her presence and my reaction remind me of so much I lack.

Your admission of such a fundamental absence underlines the role this patient is playing in forcing you to confront your repressed desires—desires that have been sadly misdirected but are nonetheless instructive. However you might choose to believe you've simply found yourself on this icy cornice, which incidentally means *edge* in Italian, the metaphor is an intellectually dishonest evasion of your subjective responsibility. You've put yourself in danger, on the edge of this icy genital void, and whether your choices have been conscious or not, you've repressed something essential in your nature that now puts you at odds with yourself and, I might add, puts your patient in grave danger.

I know, I know. But the transference-countertransference bind we're in feels unbreakable, Peter said, with what to his own ear came perilously close to a whine. I don't know how I can continue treating her with the erotic undercurrent as a dominant element during session, and I'm at a loss how to diffuse it.

You can get ahold of yourself. You have to. How are things with Alice, by the way?

Not great, he answered reluctantly.

Peter, this acting out on your part is a symptom of neglecting your personal life. The profession is rife with people just like you, but to do this work well you must be complete in yourself, without a great raft of repressed desires. You've violated that with this patient. How is your self-disclosure?

I've been circumspect, as always.

Does she know you're married—or has she asked?

She knows. My wedding announcement remains online. Beyond that, I haven't said anything. Nothing about kids or whether I'm still married. I'm a blank slate for her.

Good. I'm happy to hear it. You can get this in hand, Peter. I'm sure. And the fact that you're here, that you made the appointment to see me, is promising. Tell me about Alice.

She's just the same, really, but more so. Cold, distant, unaffectionate. We're no longer sleeping in the same bed. So there's that.

Alice has a great many schizoid traits. You knew that when you married her. And for many couples, separate beds are a reasonable arrangement. Sex?

Nope.

Have you considered couple's therapy? Enacting a fantastic tale of betrayal and vengeance with your young patient must feel good. Very, very good.

There may be an element of that. The worst of it is I'm not sure I want to change. I feel alive—excited, young, and healthy. My blood's flowing again. In some ways I'm here for my patient. I'm more worried about harming her than I am about my errors. And I don't give a damn what Alice thinks.

In that case, perhaps you should tell her.

Hardly! Peter practically snorted as he said the word.

Whatever repressed or disavowed aspect of your self that's driving the attraction, it must be quite intolerable. You've managed to keep it from yourself for quite some time. If you want to change your behavior for the benefit of your patient, fine. But if you want to continue to practice—or practice well—you'll need to recognize and tolerate these aspects of yourself. Tell Alice for the sake of your young patient. That is, if you do want to manage this—and I think you do.

I'll think about it, Peter said while thinking to himself, *I'll be damned if I tell Alice a thing about it. She doesn't deserve to know.*

As he closed the door behind him to enter the sultry heat of the late afternoon, Peter half regretted the visit. He wasn't happy with himself, true. He was weary of feeling slightly unclean. There'd been some larger shifts over the summer he hadn't discussed with Dr. March. He was aware not only of his envy of George, his annoyance with Ben, and his lust for Lisbeth but also of his boredom with his depressed patients, his deep frustration with his eating disordered patients, and an overall sense of disconnection from even his best, most entertaining patients. It wasn't the open, compassionate model that he had long strived—successfully, for the most part—to inhabit as a psychotherapist.

As he made his way back to his office, he winced as he realized that he was not the kind of doctor he would want his daughters to see. Ever. Maybe he should tell Alice? In the old days, before the girls, he had talked about his patients with her, confided in her, even sought her advice.

Alice's desire to escape her own troubling thoughts about George and Peter had propelled her work forward in recent weeks. And yet catching up had given her a more specific case of feeling left behind, the yearning to have authored ground-breaking papers, run innovative experiments, or posited one of the surprising new theories.

The Earth Institute grant application wasn't due until October but if she wanted to get back in the game she had to continue working. Winning would be a material alteration, bringing with it the things money brought while staunching the flow of her own worthlessness. Unexplained aspects of the flocking phenomenon in starlings—and other species by extension—had come a long way since she'd entered the field. Quantum biology had barely been a whisper in her department when she completed her PhD at Columbia. Now, thanks to Dr. Brian Green and Dr. Sheila Thorston, the notion that quantum mechanics could possibly begin to explain the shocking, seemingly impossible coordination of emergent phenomena in nature was almost—not quite—mainstream.

She was most excited about recent evidence of physically disconnected, nondiffusible cell-to-cell signaling. The suggestion was that photons—quantum units of light—might be the key to unraveling the communication mechanisms between birds. This was the sort of research Alice had been wanting to do for years—but she hadn't had access to the facilities. She knew she also hadn't made time. But now, getting back to the Earth Institute at Columbia was in reach; she needed one of their massive grants that came to them through the National Science Foundation, plus access to the multimillion-dollar labs and all that fabulous equipment.

Computer modeling wasn't her strong point. She was still a field biologist whose old-fashioned skills in nature as an observer and collector of data drove her research. She knew starlings tracked and remained coordinated with their nearest seven birds. But this didn't explain how they coordinated their movements. Dr. Green's work suggested the answer looked more than anything like what Einstein memorably called *spooky action at a distance.* This had been her intuition all along and now she found herself hopelessly drawn toward this risky, controversial path. It might well end in failure. Would she be humiliated? She couldn't think about that. As she wrote and revised she kept reminding herself to focus on the promising theory that the birds' eyes contained a magnetic capability called a magnetoreceptor that was communicating across space-time with the other members of the flock. Who could resist trying to prove that the ability of starlings to transmit information as rapidly as they did could be explained only by a quantum entanglement? But how to design an experiment to prove it?

Alice had been writing all morning. Peter was at the office. It had rained overnight. Riverside Drive steamed. She wouldn't have gone out, but it was time to take down the flyers, now sodden by precipitation and faded by sunlight. Many were torn, and it pained Alice to see Maebelle's face destroyed—even in facsimile. It all seemed futile after nearly ten long weeks. Maebelle must surely be dead or far, far away. Nobody would dare parade her around where desperate pleas for her return littered every surface.

Alice put on her raincoat, tucked her keys, smokes, and lighter in the left pocket, and set out to peel away her last hopes of recovering Maebelle. The hours and days had rolled forward. Here she was, walking the blocks, working on her grant application, planning their trip to Vermont, buying milk, spinach, and a big chicken to roast for dinner. As large as Maebelle loomed in her mental and emotional landscape, she'd been able to go on. The sadness had settled low in her belly where, when she thought about her, it thrashed like a trout on the rocks. But she didn't always think about it. Sometimes she went two hours without remembering. This was the cruel truth: that time heals. *Don't worry, you'll get over it. Just you wait and see.* Alice didn't want to get over it, but it was moving past her into the blurry distance no matter how hard she tried to grasp her once-fresh grief, a grief that connected her to the dog's presence.

When Alice reentered the lobby, she picked up a large package for Peter from Lorenzini (since when did he shop online—and there?) and a small, weightless brown box addressed to her. LIVE. RUSH. DO NOT FREEZE. HANDLE WITH CARE. It seemed a miracle that six hundred ladybirds could arrive in the mail just three days after she ordered them with one click on Amazon. Setting the box on the kitchen counter, Alice used scissors to carefully open the container. Inside was a mesh pouch crawling with the little orange-and-black beetles. Peter had vaguely objected to the idea of releasing six hundred bugs into the apartment, but he well knew Alice would do as she liked. Besides, they were for the most part to be released in her bedroom on the dozen plants there suffering from the scale infestation. Carefully cutting along the edge of the bag, Alice opened it and held it over her largest, most infested tree. She'd had the seven-foot-tall schefflera for ten years or more. She was determined to beat the insidious scale.

Ladybirds, as Alice liked to call them, were voracious predators. All they needed to survive was food—there was plenty of scale to gobble—and water. The plants and the beetles were ready. As the bugs dropped to the dirt, the earth in the pot came alive, the little creatures animating when their tiny legs hit soil. In moments they were marching up the trunk of the tree in orderly rows, quite literally hundreds of them reaching the first branches and in minutes busy at the tree's uppermost leaves, where they set about exploring the new growth. Before fully emptying the bag, Alice held it upright and then splayed it open over a cluster of smaller plants, knocking the remaining bugs out. The whole procedure was easy and satisfying: the beetles were already at work rescuing her tree, cleaning up the smaller plants, exploring. Some were even mating. Those settled on a leaf chewed away at the spots of scale. Alice was sure they were sucking the juice of the nasty bugs from beneath their protective shell. She hoped it was a ladybird delicacy.

Why was it that ladybirds carried none of the horror of other insects? Alice was not exceptional in her distaste for cockroaches, silverfish, mites, and spiders—among thousands of others—that inhabited urban apartments. But ladybirds were childish, innocent, and imbued with an aura of helping. Their presence felt warm and comfortable. Perhaps it was an echo of the awful nursery rhyme her mother had sung to her and she to her girls.

Ladybird, Ladybird, fly away home,
Your house is on fire and your children are gone,
All except one,
Sweet Charlotte Ann,
And she hid under the frying pan.

Peter: *Meet at Uncle Boons for dinner?*
Alice: *Sure! What time?*
Peter: *7?*
Alice: *Yum! See you there.*

Alice and Peter both ordered the frozen beer, which was no more than a frat boy trick, but it was sticky hot out, and both of them were overheated from walking across town from the 1-2-3 line. The adult Slurpee hit the spot.

They agreed on the *huu muu sawan* (pigs' ears) and *yum mamoung* (green mango salad with avocado). Peter was craving the curry beef ribs, *massaman neuh*. Alice hated greasy beef ribs, so she ordered a side of *puk fai dang* (pea shoots).

Did you get much work done today? Peter asked as the heavily pierced and tattooed waitress stepped away from the table.

I did. It went well. I think I'll make my deadline if I keep up the pace. Oh! And the ladybirds came today. They're amazing.

Oh boy, Peter said with a smile. Are they crawling around in my bed?

Of course. That's where I put them—you didn't want them? Really, they're marvelous. Marching their way to work.

They made it up the tree in two minutes, right to the tips of the leaves. What about you? How was your day?

Nothing eventful. The usual patients in and out. I think I may be tired. I was ineffectual all day—really, I've been feeling that way for a month.

Hmm. How so?

I just drift during session. Not really paying attention the way I should. It happens to the best therapists I suppose. I'm complaining because it makes the days endless. My sessions dragged. Forty-five minutes never felt so long.

Any idea what's going on? Can I help?

Nothing in particular. I guess I've been working too much. But it's almost time for August break. I'll loosen up and go back fresh in the fall.

I sometimes wonder why you weren't a neurologist or orthopedist—anything really, with some hard science behind it. You traffic in ambiguity—just listening to people talk all day must be so tiresome. I have no idea how you do it. Alice meant the comment sympathetically, but she knew it was also bitchy. She was so bored with his reluctance to talk she almost wanted to start a fight. Would it kill him to have a real, substantive conversation about what was bothering him at work after he brought it up? Always, he'd bring a thing up and then shut the topic down, as if she were the one who'd been prying in the first place.

Wow. That's quite a statement. I *traffic in ambiguity*. Is that how you see my work? Peter replied, taking an awkward bite from a great clot of slushy beer,

No, that's not what I meant—or I didn't mean to be so negative. What I meant was that your treatments are subjective

and interpersonal. That's part of their appeal—the pure humanity of what you do. Which you're good at. But your focus in
session and the quality of your response determines the value
of your work.

I don't call it subjective when a depressed patient gets
out of bed and goes back to work or when a bulimic patient
stops vomiting or a manic patient stabilizes. I'd say those are
concrete gains.

But those are the big moments. Besides, where's the
control? The patient might have gotten out of bed or stopped
vomiting or whatever whether you were there to talk to her
each Monday and Thursday—or not.

Are you trying to start a fight, Alice? I know we have
differences in the way we value our work, but knowing the
internal dynamics of a murmuration isn't exactly a service to
humanity. At least I'm attempting to contribute to the happiness and well-being of my patients.

Oh, terrific. So knowledge is useless? Good to know.
Thanks for the respect. You do always have to fight dirty, don't
you? Escalate, escalate.

The arrival of the waitress with the pigs' ears called a
truce. Peter ordered a second beer and Alice switched to a
Cruel as a Cucumber. It was, Alice reflected, almost identical to a Mrs. Dalloway with its gin, cucumber, and lime. The
difference was the Crémant d'Alsace. She wished she were
waiting for food with George, though the idea of the excitement was vaguely overwhelming.

The two of them sat blankly for some time, attempting
to deescalate by making occasional unsuccessful forays into
conversation involving Bette and Emile or their upcoming trip

to Vermont. When the rest of the food arrived, it gave them additional relief. It was less awkward to eat without conversation and their comments on the qualities of each dish made it seem almost friendly. Thank god, thought Alice, for food talk, the last refuge of the conversationally impaired.

About halfway through the meal Peter felt his phone twitch in his pocket. Relieved to have an excuse to have it in hand, he saw that the vibration was nothing more than a Twitter push notification. But why not scroll through Twitter now that he had the chance? They were hardly talking anyway.

Sorry, he said looking briefly up at Alice. I need to take care of this email. It'll just take a second.

Friday–Sunday,
July 27–29

No matter how often she witnessed it, the shocking change in the landscape as they crossed the border from New York to Vermont surprised Alice. How could one state be positively aggressive in its charm offensive and the other either oblivious or reconciled to its profoundly dreary aesthetic of postindustrial decline? The billboards didn't help. Vermont had banned them in 1968. In their place were twee wooden signs evoking the village life of a progressive state that wasn't nearly as wealthy as it appeared. Poverty in Vermont was very real, but none of it was apparent on the drive up Route 22A from Fair Haven, concealed as it was by the deceptive bucolic appeal of jelly rolls of hay dotting the green fields, white clapboard farmhouses dwarfed by massive silos, and the ubiquitous black-and-white cows appearing so peaceful and content as they grazed and chewed their cud. Not even the white plastic veal igloos lined up in the mud along the barns could mar the illusion.

Once they reached the posh Burlington bedroom community of Charlotte where Peter's parents had lived in their drafty farmhouse for the past forty years, the signals of prosperity no longer relied on the strangely convincing icons of simple farm life. No, in Charlotte bankable riches assured every chimney was repointed, board scraped and painted, collapsing barn rebuilt, and copper pot polished.

Alice dreaded visiting Peter's parents, although she wasn't certain whether the ongoing ache of missing Maebelle or the swirling mess of guilt and pleasure resulting from her tryst with George was to blame. His parents were kind, intelligent people—or they had been. Now they were defined by their age more than their accomplishments or educations. A great deal of repetition was required to carry on a simple conversation. Whatever hearing aids had been purchased at great expense over the years sat with dead batteries on their dressers. Their memories were not what they had been.

Peter's mother, Emmy, was showing unmistakable signs of mild dementia, but they weren't there long enough to experience the true effects of pretending to be interested in an anecdote for the sixth time in one day or an empty phrase repeated four times in an hour. Peter's sister, Denise, the sacrificial sibling, suffered that. She and Alice had never really gotten along. Alice had tried, initially, to make a friendly sister-in-law effort with her, but she seemed to exist in her own tightly enclosed world. She had no need or use for Alice's friendship. The determination and will for social justice that was required to run the local chapter of Legal Aid for twenty-some years had implanted a biting self-righteousness into her personality. Or maybe it had been there all along, an integral part of whatever it was that made a person get up each day, go to work, do their best, and then turn around only to do the same demoralizing work the next day—often without seeing real change. It occurred to Alice that both the Nutting children seemed to have chosen professions that were fundamentally frustrating, the results of their labors only show-ing over great stretches of time, if at all.

Alice mused as she and Peter zoomed up Route 7 in their big car, past the creeme stands, feed stores, and farm stands advertising fresh berries, corn, and, invariably, apples when it was not yet the season for them. It was as if Peter and Denise had taken on the work of changing the shape of a murmuration rather than simply understanding what it was, how it worked, and why it existed in the form it did. Perhaps it was simply the difference between research and doing what, in its most reductive form, was social work.

Peter, get me a drink, will you?

Sure, Dad. Give me a minute.

Peter hadn't so much as unloaded the groceries, and his father was demanding a drink. There was nothing surprising about this. Old Dr. Jeremy Nutting liked his bourbon. Sitting in his fine leather club chair, the room closing in on itself under the bulk of books, newspapers, and magazines, the tatty oriental rugs kept the space from looking shoddy. The effect was genteel-faded. Dr. Nutting's legs wouldn't tolerate more than a walk to the car and back. He'd done that in making his way to the driveway to greet Peter and Alice on arrival. Now he sat, waiting to have his son to himself in the chair where he was most comfortable.

In the kitchen, Peter placed a quart of organic, whole-fat plain yogurt, a loaf of wheat bread spotted with blooms of white growth, sliced turkey in butcher paper, and discolored grape-fruit juice on the kitchen counter. All of it was either visibly spoiled or long past even the most charitable interpretation of its expiration date. He needed to speak to his sister. How did she allow all this rotten food to sit in the refrigerator when his parents could easily eat it—not even noticing it had gone off? It was a tricky topic, a judgment of her attentiveness he was in no position to offer.

Denise took care of the tedious doctor's appointments, medication management, bills, and the hiring, firing, and training of caregivers, not to mention fielding endless anxious phone calls—not infrequently at 3 AM. She took them to brunch every Sunday when what she likely wanted more than anything was a day off. He would keep his silence about the rotting food. Criticizing his sister wasn't a winning proposition; she would likely throw back at him how little he did to help with their infirm parents who really, soon, needed to consider a retirement home. Of course, that would be the beginning of the end of what was their considerable retirement savings.

Can I help? Alice asked, entering the kitchen, his mother, Emmy, on her arm, the old woman's ski-pole cane in the other hand.

What are you doing, Peter? That's all perfectly good. What's the matter with it? Emmy picked up the yogurt container with her wrinkled, bony hand and squinted at it. The absence of her glasses made this examination futile—a show of interference rather than practical assistance.

Nothing, Mom. Just making room in the refrigerator.

Well, it's just so nice to have you here. It's been so long.

It was the fifth time she'd said those precise words. Her brain prompted her to articulate thoughts, and the thoughts seemed to run in tight obsessive circles. She took Peter's hand and squeezed. Peter squeezed back, meeting her eyes.

Love you, Mom. So good to see you.

Emmy, will you show me your roses? I'd love to see them. You know how much I would like a garden.

Easily distracted, the slightly stooped figure in her moth-bitten pink cardigan, nude compression stockings, and tan, poplin A-line skirt atop scuffed, brown orthopedic sneakers allowed Alice to lead her out the back to the patio, where the overgrown rose beds loosely defined the perimeter of the flag-stone, dividing the civilized leisure space of the sitting area from the functional hay pasture beyond.

Peter listened to the screen door slam and then to the sound beneath it, the *glug-glug* of the juice as it came out of the carton into the sink. To hell with recycling, he thought as he bagged the empty container with the remainder of the food from the refrigerator in a giant black plastic bag he'd tucked behind his back when his mother entered the kitchen. A jumbo box of aged Cheerios followed, along with a half-eaten box of See's nut-free chocolates and a package of gingersnaps—both leftovers from Christmas. Cinching the shiny black beast of a bag, he took it out back and stuffed it deep in the mas-sive bin, concealing the contraband beneath another bag of trash. The motion reminded him of his teen years, bagging up empties after a party and hiding them from his parents deep in this very bin. As he reentered the house he heard the tail end of his father's voice, now weaker and higher than Peter remembered it.

Peter! That bourbon! And get one for yourself.

Be right there, Dad.

Pouring his father a double with a single cube, its surface an iceberg in a honey-colored sea, he carried the heavy glass tumbler to the living room. Setting it on the coaster to the side of his father's chair, he stared at the faint vestiges of what had been a rugged, commanding face. Dr. Nutting was still almost handsome in an old-person sort of way, but the constant application of Bulleit Bourbon had eroded the finer elements, leaving pockets of deep shadow beneath his inflamed eyes and his nose redder than it should have been. The sag of the jawline suggested inattention. Or maybe it wasn't the booze. Maybe it was the eighty-five years that had done all that damage. Either way, he was rapidly moving into a new phase of physical and mental existence as he struggled to recall the titles of books he knew well, the names of friends, places he loved.

None for you? he asked. Peter watched as he brought the liquor to his lips with his shaking hand, took a sip without dribbling, and landed the glass squarely back on the coaster. The practiced action unfolded in agonizing slow motion.

Little early for me, Dad. But thanks. I'll have one with you later.

Peter would try not to have one later. He didn't like to drink booze with his father. Somehow the pretense of sobriety when he was around his father provided some distance between them, assuring Peter that he wasn't like his father, wasn't a drinker in the same way, and wouldn't turn out as he had—thinking about his first drink the moment he'd downed his coffee at 10 AM. He might have a glass of wine with Alice once his parents were in bed, but that wasn't the same.

As he sat back on the sofa, he took in the glut of photographs of his sister and sister's children in every corner. They rankled Peter, eating at every childhood insecurity of favoritism, every possible slight. It never ended. He did enjoy a mild, vengeful satisfaction knowing how angry his sister would be if she could see the pour he'd just given the old man. In fact, she'd be grabbing the glass from his hand, berating him for drinking so early in the day. To hell with her, thought Peter. It was 3 PM. Although Denise didn't forbid her father to drink, she hid the booze, meting it out in precious little drams, making a big fuss about the ritual at 5 PM—as if that would quench the insatiable thirst to obliterate the daily existence that had become intolerable to the old doctor.

Peter found his sister's need to contain their father cruel, but like the rotting food in the refrigerator, he had no standing to offer advice. He didn't get the call from his mother to come pick his father's surprisingly heavy, drunken body up off the floor if he fell. So he didn't say anything. But when his father asked him for a drink fifteen minutes after their 2:30 PM arrival, Peter wasn't going to lie to the old man, shame him into silence with a *No* as if he were a child or tell him there wasn't any whiskey in the house.

He hoped his kids would give him a fucking drink if he wanted one—whether it was 9 AM or 6 PM. If getting old was a gradual process of losing control—memory, taste, hearing, bowels, bladder, money, independence—Peter didn't want any part of it. If he wanted to drink himself to death by the time he was eighty-five, he damn well would. And if he had to, he'd hire someone who would let him. If he could.

Neither of his parents much liked Bethany, the woman who came to clean, shop, and cook once a day, but she was the best his sister could do. They had to put up with her even if Peter was sympathetic to their complaints—she refused to separate the silver from the stainless in the dishwasher, she put meat scraps in the compost, and she recycled the newspaper before they'd read it through. Peter nodded with genuine sympathy when his father groused about her, not reminding him that Bethany showed up every day without fail to change the frequently urine-soaked sheets, empty the stinking diaper pail, occasionally clean shit off their clothes before washing them, and carefully assemble bowls of cut apples, dates, prunes, and yogurt for their breakfast the next day, soup for lunch, and a sandwich or frozen entrée for dinner. The very prospect of being incapable of preparing a bowl of yogurt and fruit for himself caused a wave of despair to wash over Peter. Maybe he should have that drink—a short pour.

It had been just since Christmas; in eight months Alice saw they'd grown older at a much faster rate than previously. The laws of entropy always won. Of course, as Schrödinger had long since pointed out, aging processes weren't identical to entropy in a closed system. Alice considered the quantum phenomenological mechanisms that had been shown to effect human cells including cyclotron resonance, Zeeman resonance, the quantum Hall effect, the piezoelectric effect, and Jacobson resonance. What might be possible, hoped for, was that externally sourced non-ionizing electromagnetic fields (EMFs) could restore tissues and organs to their intrinsic electromagnetic profiles. PicoTesla range EMFs had shown real promise for their physiologic effects on memory, recall, and mental processing. But reaching beyond this, restoring biologic order in increasingly disorganized systems was the fountain of youth. This work was the stuff of science fiction. Not in her lifetime would any such treatments for degenerating cells and the resulting failure of various systems be treatable on the quantum level. It was almost funny to think about.

Peter sat on a stool at the counter across from Alice staring at yesterday's *Times*. They'd made his parents a simple pasta dinner at six, helping them with the details of going to bed as if they were children—reminding them to brush their teeth, take their medication, change the waterproof pads on the bed. This demoralizing labor wasn't pleasant, but Alice was more worn out by the nonsensical, forced cheer of conversation.

How's your dad? Did you have a good chat?

He's okay, said Peter. He's just old.

I don't know how Denise does it. Your mom was going on about the beach. The desperation of talking about the past even though you can't remember it is so sad. Is that what we'll be doing? Your parents spent summers on the Cape with the Smiths. *Do you remember the house we rented with Ernie and Barb?* We all remember it. Of course.

Hmmm, Peter half assented, pushing the newspaper aside. He didn't want to repeat a familiar conversation. He didn't want to think about how fast his parents were failing. All he could see was his own grim future. Alice wanted to talk—just talk. She had nothing particularly fresh to say. As she turned to pull down a pan from the rack behind her, he retrieved his phone from the pocket of his khakis and clicked on the big red *M* icon to open his email. Who knew what was contained in his mother's memory? Who knew what she was saving for herself? Maybe she brought up the Cape just to say something—anything—that she thought might interest them. Or maybe, all those memories had turned to goo, and all she had left was a vague impression, as flat and colorless as her description. She was just trying to hold on to it.

There was nothing sufficiently distracting in his inbox. He deleted a newsletter from the American Psychological Association, a weekly bulletin from Eater, and a notice of automated bill payment for ConEd. Closing his mail, he touched the orange, pink, and purple camera icon on his screen to open Instagram. Scrolling through his feed—too many children, pets, and food photos. None of it was sufficient to distract him. What was he looking for? Taking a sip of his bourbon, more ice melt than booze, he peeked at Alice. Her back was turned. Touching the magnifier icon to search, he quickly typed: lisbethtarkington.

Like Bette and Emile, Lisbeth mostly posted selfies on Instagram. There she was, in more graphic detail than he'd had in mind. Bikinis, slips, what appeared to be nothing but a towel. It had once seemed so strange to him, this practice of putting a picture of one's self on the internet for all to see how highly one thought of one's own appearance. What vanity it revealed and without the least tinge of shame. But his judgmental impulse had worn down. He looked forward to photos of his daughters sparkling in various flattering poses. As Lisbeth's feed filled his screen, her image sent a guilty thrill through him that wrapped around his mind, constricting the flow of any other thought.

Of course, he knew he couldn't follow her. That would be creepy and wrong. But he could lurk on the edges of her internet presence, gently stalking her visual imprint. For a brief moment he mentally checked to be sure there was no way she could know that he'd looked at her account. No. Just don't let your finger light up that outline of a heart in glowing red. Turning to lean against the kitchen counter to ensure his screen was not visible to Alice, he scrolled down Lisbeth's account.

There she was, her kittenish languor in its full glory as she posed for her own camera, always at an angle, the long hair half-hiding her fresh face. Other than selfies, she posted offbeat street shots—graffiti, a surprisingly moving dead sparrow, a view of the George Washington Bridge taken at dusk, the bridge's lights smeared into milky pearls suspended above the Hudson. He wondered how she'd achieved the effect. Jolted out of his reverie, he realized Alice was talking to him.

—start prescribing now.

Sorry, what's that? He said with a practiced, forced friendliness as he casually put his phone back in his pocket.

You know.

No.

Pills. Fentanyl, morphine, and the biggie: pentobarbital. Maybe Valium just to take the edge off before the scary drugs go down. I don't want to be like them. I want to die first.

Don't be ridiculous, Alice. Besides, it's illegal. You want me to lose my license? he said, trying to make a joke of it.

Small doses. One pill at a time, she said, sounding like a child pleading for candy.

Can we not? he said abruptly.

Okay, Mr. Shrink. Let's not talk about it. Let's ignore it. How do you feel about seeing your parents this way? Your elegant mother in diapers. Your father, paranoid and fearful, living in a whiskey-induced fever dream.

Jesus, Alice. Take it easy. They're just old. We're not them. We take better care of ourselves. It won't be the same. He was so tired of her theatrics—her need to talk when there was nothing important to say.

You're sure of that, are you? Well, I'm not. Not even a little.

Peter took his phone out of his pocket again. It hadn't even been out of his hand long enough to go dark. No longer listening, he again entered the space behind the pretty screen. He'd save the delicious Lisbeth's Instagram feed for another time. The happy flying bird icon on its sky-blue background was the only place left to go. Twitter, the adult lunch room, where photos and comments and links were a way of advertising just how damn smart and plugged in you were. Here it was most clear: the only way to value information was by its novelty. The words and images were far removed from the stale scent of frailty the house he'd grown up in had taken on, beyond reach of the smell of cheap pizza that the dried oregano in the red sauce they'd cooked for his parents' dinner had left in the kitchen, untouched by the sadness of their diminishment. Out of Alice's world.

Seething as she poured herself a glass of the slightly over-the-hill but still alive 1971 Chateau la Mission Haut-Brion that old Dr. Nutting had saved for a special occasion that never arrived—or never arrived at a moment when he still cared about drinking his most precious wine—Alice fantasized about leaving Peter. She'd been stalking studio apartments on StreetEasy. It was like shopping but not buying expensive clothes. The wine really wasn't bad, and she might as well drink it. Denise didn't give a fuck about wine, it wasn't getting any better, and besides, Peter drank what she drank. He had a right to drink it, she supposed. It belonged to his father. Her hatred of Peter for choosing his phone over her mingled with the taste of the wine's earthy layers of dirt, tobacco, and prune to form an inchoate sadness. Was she as uninteresting as all that? Lifting an old carbon steel knife from the drawer, she crushed a clove of garlic with its battered side, focusing on the bulb's acrid richness. To hell with him, she thought, if he didn't want to talk. Bastard. Or had she been insensitive? They were his parents.

Alice sautéed pork chops and cooked a pile of kelp-colored kale with the garlic. She knew she'd grown callous and overly pragmatic about old age. Her mother had died five years ago after surviving five deeply undignified poststroke years. She'd lost various faculties—balance, most of her sight, the strength in her legs. But the worst effect of the stroke had been the loss of short-term memory. Her inability to contain a chronological narrative—a conversation, a book on tape, a movie—left her afloat in her own swirling thoughts. Because she couldn't interpret and retain her world in real time, everything around her seemed unfamiliar. Isolated in her confusion, she concluded she was traveling, continually in transit. For five long years she lived her anxious existence in this state of motion, absent the knowledge of seasons and holidays, past or present, morning or afternoon. All she had was the immediate present. It was very Buddhist of her. There was nothing beyond the now. She asked for breakfast when the bowl thick with the residue of her buttered soft-boiled eggs was still in front of her; she suggested they all have a glass of wine at 10 AM; she announced she was ready for bed fifteen minutes after waking and dressing.

As an accomplished trusts and estates lawyer, the myriad indignities of her final years would have distressed and angered

her. She'd made it clear she never wanted to be incapacitated.
But even an advance directive wasn't thorough enough to prevent her doctors from keeping her alive. Her body had been
hearty and in some respects she'd been present, her long-term
memories of growing up on a ranch in Santa Rosa intact and
even much of her knowledge of the law with its grantor, set-
tlers, donors, beneficiaries, remainder beneficiaries, trustees,
codicils, perpetuities, and trusts still functional. She'd loved and
recognized her dog, an exquisitely trained standard poodle that
remained devoted to her until she'd moved to a no-pets retirement home. The dog had been put to sleep. What a whopper
that euphemism was, Alice thought, scooping the kale onto
the platter next to the pork chops.

All Alice could hear when they spoke on the phone poststroke was her own loss—her unchanged voice and lingering
sense of humor were cruel reminders of the woman she'd loved
and feared. The critical faculties that had made her presence in
full so overwhelming in life had fallen away, leaving her stub-
born body to die without a decent mind to keep track of it. Why
had they taken heroic measures to keep her alive: intubation,
aleteplase, a feeding tube that slithered in and out of the skin on
her flaccid belly, uncannily reminiscent of an umbilical cord?
Alice had disappointed her in her death as in life. She'd kept
her alive, never secured her position as a tenured professor,
and (most unforgivably) gotten pregnant at twenty-six.

She'd ended up in a glorified nursing home in St. Helena.
What was left of her estate at her death, the house Alice grew
up in having long since been sold to pay for her mother's care,
had been enough for Bette and Emile to attend the overpriced
summer school program for high school kids at Columbia and

for Peter and Alice to replace the kitchen cabinets they'd inherited when they bought their apartment fifteen years earlier. So much for the value of her mother's life, of working long days, shopping sales at Nordstrom, and flying coach. Peter's parents were about to enter the same costly zone of care. Alice didn't want to use up every asset maintaining her own extended death. She wanted to leave something for her girls. It was a waste, this hanging on to life. Her mother would have agreed if she'd been capable of agreeing to anything.

She thought of Peter's mother's remove from the garden where she had once passed long hours digging, pruning, watering, deadheading. It wasn't so important that she could no longer tend her garden—what had been lost was her personal relationship to the glorious complexity of each plant and its history as it grew, thrived, and, perhaps, died, under her care. It reminded Alice of her mother contentedly eating slabs of turkey with gluey gravy from a vat, powdered mashed potatoes, and frozen beans cooked to a state of mushy indifference. Her mother's former self would rather have starved than so much as taste the food at the retirement home that turned her body soft and round for the first time in her life. Alice practically wept watching her down the mound of macaroni and cheese that was her usual lunch choice, the starchy noodles mushed into an orange glop of cheese that tasted of salt and fat. There were worse things, Alice supposed.

The quilt in the guest room was too heavy for summer in Vermont—and ugly. Alice was afraid she was turning into a princess—cheap sheets, fleece blankets, and fiberfill pillows repulsed her. The polyester slickness of the quilt, with its embroidered cows in the foreground, a maroon barn and blot of yellow fabric for the sun in the background, was astonishingly awful. Whoever made it thought it a good idea to attach loose yarn to give the effect of cow's tails, the sun's rays, and what appeared to be birds in the sky. Alice removed the offensive item from the bed and retrieved one of the few remaining antique cotton sheets in the stack along with a light cotton blanket. Unfurling the sheet, she dreamily snapped it in the air and then guided the floating fabric over the bed into position. She then repeated the motion six times, enjoying the parachute effect of the airborne fabric as the breeze caught it, holding it aloft much longer than gravity would have normally allowed. Finally settling the sheet in place, the blanket disappointed as it flopped heavily down, lumpy and uneven, never achieving anything like the graceful height of the billowing percale. She smoothed the bed's surface and fluffed the fine old goose-down pillows, their pinstriped encasements yellowing. You couldn't buy pillows so light and fine anymore—well, Alice supposed, you could buy them, but they wouldn't be just pillows. A decent feather pillow was now a luxury—a hundred bucks or more. Maybe these were eider? She should grab a few from the house when Peter and his sister sold it. That would be tricky. Somehow the act of caring for the parents made Peter's sister owner and proprietor of the house and its contents. She would have first pick of all the art, books, pots, dishes, old carbon steel knives, green depression glasses, Anchor measuring cups and bowls, the colorful Italian Vietri pottery they'd collected on their travels—even the family photographs would be hers to claim first.

To hell with it, thought Alice, hating herself for coveting any of the things she would likely not have purchased had she discovered them in an inexpensive antique store. She didn't need more things—although her girls would. It would be only five years or so before they'd want pots, pans, silverware, mugs, glasses, and bowls, not to mention furniture. None of it was worth much—its value was in the patina of its use by Peter's parents, with their connection to it. Even if the armchairs were better quality than you'd buy in most places the girls could afford to go, it was the layers of time that inhered in the fabric, frame, and stuffing that made them worth keeping.

Having entered that state when familiar objects were falling away from them, Bette and Emile's sentimentality was a fine film that clung to anything they'd used as children. When they encountered once-familiar objects after time away, they noticed them afresh. Things evoked memories of times and places and with those memories feelings that so easily adhered to objects or clothing. Alice had once expressed a similar nostalgia to her own mother for a vase; rather than acknowledging or probing the memory, she'd snapped that such feelings were out of place in young people. Alice observed a similar impulse in Bette and Emile with sorrow. Nostalgia for what was commonplace at home was a marker of growing up and away. Escaping the familiar, however invisible this landscape might once have been, was one of the first losses as the simplicity of childhood fell away.

The parking lot at the Philo Ridge Farm, a market and café in Charlotte, might have been The Palm's in East Hampton. Peter cringed at the transformation of the space even as he admired the lines of the immaculately renovated structures. Last he'd seen the place it had been a sorry cluster of farm buildings defined by dirty sheep grazing over stubby fields, broken-down tractors parked in the rutted lane next to the collapsed classic red barn, and antiquated threshers left to rust in the abandoned feedlot. Now it was shiny: wildflowers, neat hay bales, and newly pointed stone walls outside and polished tables, high ceilings, and exposed beams inside. From top to bottom it was all very geothermal, solar, organic, sustainable, humane, holistic—what else was there? Peter wanted to like it but couldn't begin to.

It was a good thing to support the area's farmers. The four hundred acres of farmland had been preserved and the store they'd built next to the restaurant sold local produce, meat, broth, and even hand-dyed yarn. But the smugness of it rankled. When did fresh, local fava beans, sheep's-milk cheese, and a decent loaf of bread become a religious experience?

Peter thought of Marx's insights into commodity fetishism, how *the religion of sensuous appetites* distorted human relations as well as the intrinsic value of things themselves, turning a humble fava bean into a triumph of agroconscious gourmet consumerism. That the sexual element of a fetish wasn't made explicit didn't make it invisible, he reflected as he entered the precious space, moving his eye over the curved lines of hand-hewn maple, plump ripe fruits, scantily clad consumers, and nubile young counter help. The place wasn't a store or a restaurant; it was a shrine where one worshipped the goods and purified oneself by buying and eating.

So they ate. Well, Alice had a *farm-fresh* latte and a slice of *heritage* peach from a sample plate. Peter tried to quell his annoyance as he stood reviewing the menu with his parents. They could read it, but it was difficult for them to focus on the items, to make sense of what was offered.

Black Garlic Sausage with Heirloom Field Peas, Peter read. Hmmm. Field peas as opposed to . . . ? Never mind, Dad. Let's see, *Crunchy Vermont Wood Chanterelles with Soft-Scrambled Philo Ridge Araucana Eggs.*

Crunchy mushrooms? And what the hell is an Araucana? Sounds reptilian, his father replied.

Yes, well, Dad, It's all a little silly. Let's see what else there is. *Black Tartarian Oat Scone with Brambleberry Jam,* he read. Peter really had had about enough of the menu. Between the pedigree of every grain and the word *brambleberry?* Really? There was no such thing. Berries grew in brambles but . . .

Never mind, Peter, his father said, as if reading his mind. I'll have eggs. And a black coffee.

Emmy, how about the granola? It has coconut and you can order it with a peach and yogurt? Alice offered. What the menu actually said was *Hulless Oat and Grafton Maple Granola with Fair Trade Coconut and Hinesburg Black Walnuts. Served with Philo Ridge white doughnut peaches or low-bush blueberries.* She looked over at Peter, who was helping his father. What a mistake. It was crowded—they'd had to wait while a large family, long since finished eating, perused their phones in silence unaware or not caring that two elderly people were standing three feet away waiting for a table. They finally ordered and, after some awkwardness, settled on the long benches.

Okay, Peter said as the food arrived. Success! Taking a bite, he added cheerfully: My pizza is very good. Can't beat a wood-fired oven even if we city people claim coal burns hotter.

Reminds me of college. Pizza for breakfast. How's yours, Mom? She appeared bewildered, pushing the mixture before her around in the big bowl. She finally took a tiny bite.

This is very good yogurt. My goodness. And what a peach. Alice, have a bite. You're not eating anything? You should eat something.

Thank you, Emmy. I'm very happy with my coffee. It's so good to be here with you both. I'm sorry we have to rush off back to the city so quickly. We promise to come again, soon. Right, Peter?

Absolutely. We'll be back in the fall. For a much longer visit. How does that sound? In a couple months. You've got a birthday coming up, Dad. Big eight five. That calls for a party.

No party, he said firmly. How's your practice Peter? Busy? He'd already asked Peter about his practice a dozen times. It didn't matter. They were almost out the door, headed back to their own lives.

Great, Dad. Everything's going really well. I'm too busy.

And the girls? How are my granddaughters? I wish they were here.

Why aren't they here? asked Emmy in some confusion, as if their absence had just occurred to her.

They're both loving California, Mom. I guess I shouldn't be surprised. Such New Yorkers and yet California can steal you away. The light. The air. The space. They've really fallen for Berkeley.

They'll be home soon? she asked, as if they were in some peril.

Yes, home for Labor Day. But a short visit. I'm hoping to convince them to be home next summer. I don't know how we agreed to let them stay away this summer. It was just such a great opportunity. Both of them are interested in environmental studies, so working on solar in California is a dream job for them.

You've got to let them loose, Peter's father said. Just let them go. Best thing for them. Now Peter, he was home, home, home, he said, turning to Alice. And I don't think it did him much good. UVM is so close he came home on weekends.

To do laundry, Peter added.

You mean to have you do his laundry, Alice said with a smile looking at Emmy.

Ah, but I didn't mind. Never minded. Not for my Peter.

Peter looked fondly at his mother, his rage at the self-important food, people, and space melting into nothing as he looked at her, reminded by the glimmer of her old self in her affectionate words what a truly wonderful presence she'd been in his life. How solid. Always, she'd adored him without a hint of criticism. To her, he was perfect and always had been.

The conversation reminded Alice of scrubbing menstrual blood out of Bette's and Emile's lacy underwear throughout high school. At the time, it had surprised even her that she did it with no hint of disgust. Alice had been ashamed of how squeamish she'd been when she'd cleaned up after her own mother. She'd noted that Denise had none of this with her mother and father: she'd take a bite of their half-eaten sandwiches, drink from the same glass, and handle the wet diapers without appearing to mind in the least. Alice would never have taken a bite of Emmy's yogurt—or her own mother's—even if she'd wanted some. It was as if death and age had somehow tainted them.

As Alice cleared the plates and glasses, she considered her own failings. There was a self-protectiveness about her that she didn't like but didn't seem able to cure. She handed Emmy her sporty cane and offered her arm to steady her. The frail woman rose, her food barely touched, and as she stood straight, securing her balance, Alice found herself leaning and kissing the velvety skin of her powdery cheek.

Wednesday, August 8

To make matters worse it was the hottest day of the summer—
98 degrees and 86% humidity. Alice was melting; she knew
her swampy crotch and armpits were teeming with bacteria,
redolent in their glorious medium. She bought a baby-size soft
vanilla ice-cream cone with rainbow sprinkles from a Mister
Softee truck parked on 20th Street. Licking the sprinkles, she
seethed as she made her way up 5th Avenue past the midlevel
retail, liking nothing about the ice cream beyond its tempera-
ture on her tongue. She'd once adored a street cone but they
were never as good as she remembered. Still, an ancient taste
memory kept tempting her back.

Why had she agreed to meet George for lunch? Via direct
message on Facebook he'd said he must see her. It seemed
too awkward to ask why, and she was far too polite—not to
mention undisciplined—to say no. She'd been unsuccessfully
endeavoring to erase him from her mind for two months; it
didn't help that she continued to dip a guilty foot in the unruly
memory when it suited her. Seeing him would likely freshen
the images. Finally, though, it was her eagerness to discover

what would unfold that drove her forward; she'd submitted to the momentum of the event as if fate's gloved hand were urging her toward a fixed destiny.

They'd met at the Union Square Cafe. Fortunately it was well out of her neighborhood, far from Peter's office. She'd dressed with the meticulous care of a teenage girl in a new Stella McCartney sleeveless black jumpsuit with Maryam Nassir Zadeh chunky-heel sandals. As soon as she'd hit the street the jumsuit had felt like a mistake. Who wore black in this weather—even if it was sleeveless linen?

Alice had never seen herself very accurately, but the truth was she bordered on heroin chic—so thin as to be unhealthy but with a tan, mascara, and a dim outline of her favorite Dior lip liner, she looked much healthier than the term suggested. She wore her clothes like a model, her body one long Tony Viramontes line. Everything looked good on her.

At the sight of George waiting at the bar, Alice's breath had caught. For a moment, afraid, she'd even considered turning around and slipping back out the door before he saw her. But he had seen her. Rising, he'd greeted her with his memorably charming smile. Then she'd detected an immediate coldness that had put her on guard. Of course he had an agenda— why else would he have insisted they meet? Getting dressed, she couldn't help fantasizing that he needed to see her again because he couldn't forget about her and simply had to take her down the street to the W, peel off her clothes, and lay her down on the bed. She hadn't made up her mind yet if she'd agree to go. No, the moment she caught sight of his slightly stiff shoulders she'd known that was not what he had in mind. But why else, really, had she come? She didn't need more rejection—she got all she needed from Peter. She'd grown used to the illicit place George occupied in her mind. She could always visit, finding there consistent proof of her desirability, however Peter might ignore or demean her.

You look well. Thank you for coming, he'd said, still standing.

Not at all. Good to see you. Alice had wondered how the greeting would go. They were rather past a handshake, but a peck on the cheek seemed awfully chummy, and a hug was, well, simply too close to falling into each other's arms. There would be no touch, Alice had quickly realized, somewhat shocked at the turn things had taken.

I hope I haven't ambushed you. I don't blame you if you were hesitant to come, and I really don't want you to get the wrong idea, he'd said, pulling out a stool at the bar for her.

No—And then she'd stopped herself. Why lie? Why make him comfortable at her own expense? She'd started again. Let's say I was curious. I wasn't sure it was a good idea—for so many reasons. Was she teasing him? Flirting. She really had no idea. It had been so long since she'd tried to flirt with anybody she wasn't sure what it looked like anymore.

I know. It probably isn't. He'd laughed. Let me get right to it. I wanted to tell you how sorry I am about what happened.

I'm not sure I know what you mean. Alice's surprise had been real and complete.

I know it's awkward, but I wanted to be sure you didn't feel I'd been too—er—forward.

Perhaps I should be asking you the same? I don't see why you would think that. Alice had recovered herself, but she hadn't been sure if she felt sad, humiliated, or angry.

We'd been drinking. Those gin drinks. What were they called? George had said, attempting to conspiratorially meet her eye. Alice had ignored the look and the question. Had he truly forgotten the name of the drink or was the question a false assertion of his indifference?

Yes, the important part of that statement is that we both had been drinking, Alice had said with emphasis. She then pushed the barstool back in place indicating she wouldn't be sitting down.

Yes, but . . .

But what? Alice had surprised herself. A feeling that might have been mere annoyance had blossomed into a something much more forceful at the idea that she was a victim. What she recalled as a seductive evening, one of the most memorable and sensuous sexual encounters she'd ever experienced, had been spun as worse than a casual mistake. George not only wasn't here to take that pleasure for another spin; he was here to express his regret and cover his tracks.

I'm so relieved, he'd said. Still standing, his posture had returned to the natural, cocky ease of a good-looking man as he'd observed Alice reject the stool. The painful interview was almost over.

Why? Why are you relieved? Do I look pitiable and weak to you? Alice was suddenly quite pleased she'd worn black. Her clothes felt powerful.

I'm sorry. I don't mean to insult. I really am sorry if I've offended you in any way. I just wanted to be certain. And to apologize.

For what? For fucking me? For allowing me to fuck you back? She couldn't believe she'd said it. The woman over

George's shoulder stared with the look of prissy indignation you'd give to someone talking during a movie. She'd surprised even herself with her crass directness. Perhaps all the years of verbal sparring with Peter had done her good.

I'm not unhappy you see it that way, he'd said. Really. It's just that I've started therapy—I know it's ridiculous but there it is—and I've been trying to work through what I'll call, for lack of a better term, seductive behavior. I pursued you for reasons that aren't, perhaps, the right ones. I'm concerned that I wanted something and that I used you to claim it.

For Christ sake, she'd said, exasperated. What are the right ones? Do you think my motives were unpacked before I decided to have a drink with you, before I spent three hours talking to you, before I chose to leave the bar with you, before I closed the goddamn door to the hotel room behind me with you practically straddling me, my pants undone, my shirt half off? You know, women actually like sex, too. Maybe I used you. Has that occurred to you? Maybe I should be apologizing to you for luring you to the hotel for my own dark, impure purposes.

I think you know that's not the case, he'd said, as if insulted by the idea. Alice hoped the silence that followed communicated indifference and hauteur—not confusion or regret.

I'll tell you what, George. Let's just leave it at that. You've said you're sorry—do you feel all better? She hadn't been able to help one taste of unnecessary, childish sarcasm but hoped she hadn't shown too much. She hoped she'd appeared cool—as if this thing were nothing and she'd come downtown for just another fuck. There would be no crying over lost dogs or anything else today. Alice had taken her purse from the edge of the chair where she'd hung it. She hadn't even had time to cool off in the frosty, hushed air of the perfectly appointed, flower-festooned space.

Don't go, Alice. Please. I've been clumsy. You've misunderstood.

Have I? And with that she'd given him what she hoped was her most dismissive shrug, turned, and left.

Licking the last of the garish sprinkles from the creamy white ice cream, she considered. Perhaps she'd been too hard on him. He'd been trying to do the right thing. But now the whole encounter, the lovely memory of it, was spoiled. Now she almost hated him. Why couldn't he have been more careful, maybe slowly listened to her? Why did he assume she lacked agency, will, desire, and her own motives? How dare he assume he'd outmatched her? Well, she thought, violently chucking the remainder of the cone in the trash and fishing for a cigarette in her purse, he hadn't.

Alice stood smoking as a woman with marvelous legs walked past, her heels elongating her calves while giving definition to the gastrocnemius. Alice observed how, in New York City, you couldn't tell a woman's age by her legs or the length of her skirt. Time and again she had admired a particularly muscular, toned pair of legs from behind—a runner? A lucky twentysomething gym rat, she'd think, only to discover when she saw the woman's face how old she was. Never mind the $400 jars of night cream—the face told the truth. There it was again as the woman turned to cross the street: the pinched look of the cosmetically carved and the skin no better than her own. It was as if someone had attached the wrong head to a gorgeous body.

Looking down at her own tan feet, she took the summer months in the city as an anatomy lesson. Everyone's skin continually on display—shoulders, bellies, legs, arms in every shade of white, brown, and black. Alice still wore shorts and strappy tops; for a while she thought the world had grown more polite as catcalls no longer caught her mid-stride. Feminism at work. Until one day Bette and Emile complained about the men on Broadway and how they couldn't walk a block without hearing whistles and *God bless you, baby* or *My you're fine, girl*. Alice only then realized her error. It was both deeply sad and an immense relief. How liberating to no longer be the object of the insatiable male gaze; how devastating not to be seen.

Maybe, she thought, chucking her cigarette butt into the street with a hard downward thrust, a street dog would be more satisfying than the shitty ice cream. So much for lunch.

Hot dog in hand, she pushed back the foil as she used her finger to run a bit of sweet relish down the length of the wiener next to the shiny strip of ketchup. Why take what had been nothing but pleasure and compress it into a tiny ball, as one might this piece of foil, compacting it into a hard wad of nothingness? Wonderfully, Alice knew the foil would collapse with a kind of predictable certainty as the length of creases followed a state variable. Thinking about it eased her mind, allowing the memory of that almost-long-ago evening with George to return. She'd been drawing on it as a source of energy, as if it were a glowing, radioactive isotope. Now it had been spoiled by the depressingly ordinary morality that took over when conformist impulses met disorderly behavior. Couldn't anything remain unexamined? How sick she was of it all, how disgusted with herself for misreading him as sophisticated enough to allow a thing to simply be what it was.

* * *

Peter had a free hour in his day, a gift from Ben, who had canceled his appointment that morning. What a fine thing to be paid without doing any work! And then there was the guilty relief of escaping Ben. As he ushered his 1 PM patient out the door he pondered what to do with the unexpected bounty. Self-indulgence was always an option; it was tempting to slip around the corner for a big, greasy cheeseburger and fries. But he was behind on billing, and it was almost the first of the month when he handed discretely folded bills to patients detailing visits, charges, and payments received.

Compromising with himself, he ordered a cheeseburger, fries, and a Coke on Seamless and then settled in at his desk to enter credits into patient accounts. As he tallied George's bill, he thought about their session earlier that week. His patient was struggling with his sexual infidelity. At Peter's prompting, they'd further discussed the significance of his father's role in his current behavior. George wasn't a pretty boy for nothing. Beyond the five women he admitted to, what had emerged was a lengthy history of seductive behavior.

I'm just very physical, he'd said. I don't think of it as sexual behavior; I'm a toucher. I've become more aware of how often I put a hand on a colleague's or student's back, arm, or shoulder. It's harmless—almost an extension of hand gestures, a kind of communication. I don't touch women only because I want to sleep with them—not at all. It's just the way I am. You know, *touchy*. I think I have a pretty good sense of which women object or misinterpret me. But like I said, in the past year I've been jolted into awareness of the dangers. Two weeks ago during mandatory sexual harassment training for faculty I felt like everyone in the room was staring at me when they discussed touching as a flirtatious, suggestive, potentially coercive act. There's now a no-touching policy in place! I suppose it's suspended in a crowded elevator—what do you think?

Has anyone ever asked you not to touch them?

Absolutely not. My female colleagues are my friends—we used to sling an arm over each other's shoulder, high-five, and even hug once in a while—to celebrate or if someone just needed a hug. I did the same with my male colleagues. Nobody ever indicated discomfort.

Perhaps your graduate students, for example, wouldn't feel comfortable speaking up. It might be awkward for them to complain.

I've always had excellent relationships with my grad students. We spend hours and hours together. We eat together at the lab. Sometimes we even sleep there when we have a lengthy protocol running.

Have you ever had sex with one of your graduate students?

Well . . . George had paused, flushing. I have, a long time ago. But it wasn't what it sounds like. She pursued me, I can assure you. Beautiful girl. And there were no hard feelings. Of course, I'd never do it today. I could lose my job. I don't exactly resent the policy. But the emphasis on women's voices, on believing women no matter what their complaint or accusation, strikes me as an overreaction to a very real problem. Weinstein was a rapist, and I hope he rots in jail. But Louis C.K. never touched anybody. I mean, jerking off in front of women without asking first—or did he ask? I guess it was just Sarah Silverman who told him fine, fire away! Anyway, I find myself constricted and uncomfortable now, but that's as it should be, I suppose. I see how my casual way of touching might be seen as flirtation and that women under me might feel compelled to respond—

Do you believe the student you had sex with, by virtue of your position of authority over her, never could be fully free? Would you agree your perception of her pursuit of you, as you tell it, might have been distorted by your privilege and power? Or perhaps it simply felt safer or easier for her to go along with what she perceived as your flirtatious behavior?

Dr. Nutting, are you judging me? Really. I thought that wasn't the protocol here. Aren't you supposed to listen? he'd said with a disarming grin.

I am listening. Of course. But I'm also hearing you equivocate. I'm taking your statements and applying them to your actions. The comfort of generalities, of agreeing with general principles, is open to everyone. But applying those principles to ourselves, living by them, signals honesty and integrity. Much of what I do here—however successfully—is based on the premise of honesty. It's an essential feature of the therapeutic process, not just between patient and doctor but in the private lives of each. Integrity isn't a thing that others can see or even know from looking or talking to a person. Integrity is private—only you can know if you are living with integrity.

You're quite a fan of that word.

I think it's a complicated and useful word, one that helps to pinpoint some of the qualities I believe make people happy. You've come here because you're struggling with a disjunction between what you believe is right and your actions. If you believed cheating on your wife and lying to her were ideal behaviors, you wouldn't be here. But you don't.

I am ashamed of my behavior.

I'm not suggesting you should be, so we're clear. And I don't think shame is useful. Rather, understanding the pattern of your behavior and where the incongruities exist between what you desire for yourself and what you have is useful.

You know, I've been thinking a lot about my father and how he made my mother suffer. So the other night I dug out a photo album to get a better feel for that time. Who was I then? What did I look like? There was a snapshot of him with my mother and his cake: *Happy 44!* I'm in the photo wearing the varsity letter jacket I was wearing on the bus the day I saw him coming out of the steak house—it was a big deal for me, that jacket. I lost it at a party that same year. I looked so young in the photo, so innocent. And yet I knew. That was when I knew he'd been cheating on her. The moment, the outfit, the smell of the crowded bus on a rainy day, all of it is frozen in time for me.

Peter had listened, and doing a little simple math realized George had begun his own infidelity at the same age, a decade ago. According to George's intake he would have been forty-four when he slept with his grad student—the same age his father had been when young George became conscious of his father's cheating. Peter wondered when—or even if—George would recognize the unhappy convergence. How strange and wonderful the mind is, how marvelously entwined this universe of things and the concordance of time and space. That George's subconscious mind could hold the memory of his father's age, keeping it all those years deep in the substrata of the neurons allocated to hold long-term memory, only later to signal him to behave as he did precisely at the right moment was a marvel. George seemed to have no conscious awareness of knowing his age at the time of his first affair, but his subconscious hadn't forgotten. This was part of what Peter loved about his work: the long reach of the past, the machination of the subconscious exerting its force on the present. But George had to see it himself. Peter could help to lead him there, but it would be a slow process, one in which he would need to acknowledge the potent, subterranean forces driving his actions.

Well, time's up for today, Peter had said, glancing up at the clock.

Thank you, Dr. Nutting, George had replied with a sly smile. I will ponder my integrity.

And on that note George had left his office. It had been a mixed but rigorous session. Looking back on it, Peter was surprised by his own lecturing. It wasn't like him to force a point as he had, but something about George's easy sense of entitlement had compelled him to speak. Or was it something else? There was his own behavior with Lisbeth and its murky status. Knowing was difficult, but change was a phantom. As he tallied bills and entered dollar amounts into his billing system, it flashed on him how much the session had been about him—not George.

The therapeutic action put demands on him as the analyst that he was increasingly having trouble handling. Peter needed to slow down. It was almost as if his own impatience were getting the better of him lately. He was projecting his frustration with himself onto his patients. It was countertransference run amok. Perhaps, as Dr. March had said, it was time to get back into therapy himself. Did he, as Dr. March had suggested, want to blow his life up? Of late, blinkering himself to the myriad discordances between his own beliefs and behavior had become his most pressing mental occupation—second only to actively daydreaming about Lisbeth.

Friday–Sunday,
August 10–12

It was nice having rich friends. Friends with houses—compounds—on the beach in Sagaponack. Alice packed carefully, meditatively pressing her favorite crisp cotton blue-and-white sundress she'd bought at the Barneys Warehouse sale years ago, filling her weekend bag with linen shorts and camisoles, casual leather sandals, a straw hat, and three bathing suits. Why everyone was so proud of packing light she had no idea—better too heavy than too light. All she had to do was carry the bag to and from the car. Who cared if it weighed fifteen, twenty, or thirty pounds? Even so, three swimsuits did seem excessive, but the Emilio Pucci bikini, with its white, pink, and orange color-block design, had the distinction of being her favorite and the most expensive. Alice wasn't about to spoil it by exposing the fabric to the corrosive effects of salt or chlorine; it would be her sunning suit; the fabric hugged her body, covering the crucial areas as concisely as her best La Perla bra-and-underwear set. The practical Norma Kamali navy one-piece was for swimming in the pool or sea, and the

Dolce & Gabbana retro, high-waisted floral bikini with a bra top was fine for walking but she didn't really need it. She threw it in anyway.

The standard summer offering of half a case of Domaines Ott Bandol had been supplemented with three pounds of smoked salmon from Barney Greengrass along with bialys, bagels, and cream cheese. It was the least they could do. The weekend would be an indulgence, and Marina Turing and Catherine Block were among their oldest friends. The two had been together for as long as they had. Alice had met Marina at Columbia where Marina was in the MFA program for creative writing. Unlike her classmates, she'd become the rarity that is a financially successful novelist. When the first bestseller, her third novel, yielded hundreds of thousands, it had seemed like more money than she knew what to do with, and Marina had been giddy with excess as she shopped for things she'd never been able to afford. From that moment on she always picked up the tab when out with friends. It was quite a reversal from her Housing Works wardrobe and alligator arms of times past.

Then the money just kept coming—a new novel, another option, a film premiere, and the frenzied sale of more *eunuchs*, as she jokingly referred to units of sale. Her name was everywhere, but surprisingly she'd managed to resist becoming self-important. After a brief period of confusion over what to do with all the money once she had a nice watch, clothes, and furniture, she bought a bunch of real estate, upgraded her car, and started traveling a lot and in style. Beyond the decoration, she was the same, changed by motherhood far more than by sudden riches.

Marina and Catherine had met in college. They were what Alice thought of as a permanent couple—so interdependent you couldn't have one without the other. Catherine wasn't particularly successful at anything other than raising a kind, intelligent, curious daughter, maintaining a partnership for more than a quarter decade, and tastefully spending Marina's money. Fortunately for the couple, she wasn't a writer and she wasn't ambitious.

What a gift that would be, thought Alice as Peter pulled onto the first stretch of the Southern State Parkway, to be contented to raise her daughters, garden, decorate the house, and shop for pretty things. Catherine's flawless taste gave their lives the polish and glamour money alone couldn't confer. She curated their lives with exacting care while not needing much of anything for herself. Somewhere within her there was wisdom—or perhaps a deep sense of resignation—that enabled her to inhabit the wealth she'd lucked into without questioning her dependency or bothering with the fact that she was always second when she entered a room. It was always Marina, Marina, Marina—fans wanting selfies, interviews, followers on every platform, invitations, and honors. But happily for everyone, Catherine's indifference to it all was complete. Alice believed she would have been destroyed by such an obvious imbalance of power. She fought to avoid inadvertently filling herself with Peter's tastes, his agenda, the very tone of his worldview. The status of her professional life weighed on her. Was it fame she wanted? Yes, the limited but very real fame of being a known name in her field, of being invited to deliver papers at MIT, Caltech, and Oxford, to give a TED Talk, and to head prize committees. But she would settle for feeling solidly accomplished;

she wanted her gifts validated. She wanted to be what some lightly refer to as successful.

With the legalization of same-sex marriage, Marina and Catherine had organized their decadent beachfront wedding in Sagaponack around a massive Maine lobster boil and clambake. Two hundred local oysters on the half shell started a party that ended with an eight-tier, nasturtium-festooned lemon poppy seed cake with elderflower buttercream. The long dining tables, set on platforms on the beach had been impressively laid out with seagrass chargers on tablecloths the color of the ocean at dusk, the napkins mirroring the whitecaps visible beyond the shoreline. It had been a gusty day that whipped the women's long hair into their eyes and stole everyone's hats, but so warm and lively that the blown sand and violent wind seemed almost intentional—part of the majesty of it all.

Bette and Emile had been included in what was otherwise an adult event. Throughout the day they'd clung to Sam, Marina and Catherine's daughter, their wild energy and easy chatter focused on the smallest pleasures that day—the digging of the big hole to cook the clams, the live lobsters someone set loose on the beach. Paired with their honest play in sand and surf was a memory supplanted by the nearly adult presences all three girls now inhabited. Alice loved Sam well enough to be genuinely happy with her acceptance at Yale without the feeling being spoiled by envy or jealousy. She was sorry she wouldn't have a chance to catch up with her this trip. She, like Bette and Emile, was far away, building the foundations of her own distinguished life.

Alice had loved the summer family time—all of them at the beach, the girls' long hair impossibly tangled from salt water and wind, the hollows of their ankles caked with sand, their slim prepubescent bodies gangly and awkward as they giggled, talked, and argued, the metal brackets of their braces packed with corn from the pile of gnawed cobs at the center of the table. Alice wished all of it back.

She and Peter stopped for lunch at the Bayside Clam Bar and Grill in East Islip, an annual ritual en route to Sagaponack that once again reminded her of coaxing five-year-old Bette and Emile to taste the succulent, sweet fried clams when all they wanted to eat was chicken fingers, fries, and ketchup. After ordering two baskets of clams and two beers through the tiny window, Alice headed toward the picnic tables to find a seat where she could almost taste the nearby ocean while feeling the sand between her toes. But Peter objected. He hated the heat but the direct sun was the greatest affront to his comfort. He'd never enjoyed eating outdoors. A picnic—even seated at a table, which hardly counted—was his idea of hell. Just as Peter had decided he hated eating outdoors, Alice supposed she had attached herself to the idea of the pleasure of sitting outside as much as to its reality—but attached she was. So they stubbornly ate apart, Peter indoors, where the TV was tuned to CNN, and Alice outdoors, where she found herself tearing up at the ridiculous lonely dissolution of what had once been a family ritual.

Had it ever been the way she remembered? Or were fights over chicken fingers and Peter's irritation at eating outdoors the true content of the memories she clung to? It was as if her airbrushed version of events was founded on carefully edited images compiled from hours of film shot over the course of twenty years. Maybe she would look back on the failure of this very lunch fondly, even longingly, as she now looked back on previous visits. What a gift that would be.

Using her half-full bottle of Coors Light to weigh down her mostly empty paper basket, the full serving of fries scattered cold and stiff on its greasy surface, she managed to tear off a bit of napkin from the metal dispenser on the table to wipe her eyes. She then wandered down toward the docks. A furtive cigarette was a surprisingly effective antidote to her rage—or was it sadness she was feeling?

The house was more sculpture than dwelling. In realtor speak, the *modern style offered at 719 Daniels Lane epitomized indoor/ outdoor living, with floor-to-ceiling windows masterfully designed to ensure views of the breaking ocean waves that are elegantly framed and captured from every room in the home.* The steel bulkhead and extensive drainage system meant it didn't matter if the waves washed over the grounds in winter, the briny, dirty ocean water flooding the pool, jacuzzi, and lawn. Nothing leaked. Nothing broke. Global warming be damned.

Marina and Catherine had now been in possession of too much money long enough to not be embarrassed by it. Rather than fussing over or hiding their riches, they chose to be generous. Alice would have liked to be so liberal. What a nice feeling it must be to offer so much, so easily. Arriving at the usual hour of four-thirty closer to five—nobody wanted guests before cocktail hour—they settled their bags in the spare, elegant bedroom and headed out to the ocean for a swim.

Marina looked good. Her hair now white blonde and short, she'd morphed into a more androgynous version of herself over the years, with the soft waifishness of a boy defining her slim limbs and petite waist. Catherine was stylish and much harder looking, with close-cropped dark hair and a muscular masculinity that contrasted with fluid warmth and ease.

Post-swim, Alice nibbled macadamia nuts, rice crackers, and artichoke tapenade by the pool with Marina. They caught up between sips of a very fine 2017 Domaine Ferret Pouilly-Fuissé. Catherine had gone for a run, and Peter had retreated to their room for a *rest*—which meant looking at his phone and waiting until it was time to have a martini. He would reserve his charm for later, when they were all together.

I'm sorry, so sorry, about Maebelle. When Peter told me you wouldn't be bringing her I was so sad. Who didn't love Maebelle? How are the girls? It must be hard on them, so far away.

Actually, we haven't told them.

Really?

Not yet. I need to tell them in person. It feels wrong over the phone.

Was it sudden?

Sudden? What do you mean?

I'm sorry. I'm sure it's not something you want to talk about. Let's not.

No, it's okay, Marina. I probably should talk about it. Peter's no help.

How are you two? Seemed a little tense when you arrived.

You know. Or maybe you don't. You always seem blissfully happy. Still crazy in love?

It seems so.

Alice considered that if she spent her summer in this house she might be happier in her marriage, too. She quashed the inevitable tinge of envy, recognizing that being married to a woman wasn't the same as living with your best friend—which was what she instinctively supposed her lesbian friends enjoyed. Such relationships likely came with the same annoyances she mistakenly identified as particularly male. And it wasn't for nothing that there was an acronym for the notorious absence of sex in female relationships—LBD, lesbian bed death.

Well . . . we're okay. Same as ever. I miss the girls. How's life without Sam?

We're getting on, and Sam's great—she loves New Haven. It was tough at first. Catherine started therapy in September. Seems to be helping—she was devastated. You know me, I always have my work. I made sure I had a book due last fall. It saved me but made things worse for Catherine. I'm a bit nervous about her therapy—

Couples always are and have a right to be, Alice said

Yeah. I've known so many couples who broke up after one of them started treatment. All of a sudden they work it all through, decide they're trapped, that they need to realize themselves, and then they break free.

It can be pretty destructive. Catherine is likely too smart for that. And I hope the shrink is good enough not to encourage it. As you know, most shrinks are worthless—and those are the good ones, Alice said with a laugh.

You're so bad, Alice. I respect the hell out of Peter. I know you do, too. He's the model I set my standard by. I've just seen so many people fucked up—or waste their money.

Absolutely. Peter is always going on about the decline of his profession. What with CBT and pharmaceuticals, you're lucky to find a well-trained analyst, and even then it's not easy finding someone good.

You know, I think it's a calling, Marina agreed.

Like the priesthood—when that meant something beyond filth! Maybe teaching is a better analogy? You know those teachers who are meant to teach—driven to it the way you're driven to write?

It doesn't help that I'm afraid Catherine will fall for the woman. I googled her—she's positively hot!

You're not so bad yourself. She's not going anywhere.

So, really. How are you and Peter? Empty nest. It's a big adjustment.

I don't know, Catherine. We're in it for the long haul. So what if we haven't had sex in years—sex is so twentieth century. I can't believe I'd ever find anyone else if I left Peter. Or if I snuck around, think of the mess I'd make. How do you know a person? I'm so used to Peter. I trust him. He loves me. I love him—whatever the hell that means. What else do I need? Passion? I could hardly breathe when I first met Peter. I couldn't think about anything else. I wouldn't want that feeling again—even if I could have it.

Have you given up having sex? Are you never having sex again? You can't, Alice. You're hardly over fifty.

Nobody said forever. It's a phase. We'll figure it out. For now, I'm fine with it. I have my ways. What about you?

It's been a little uneven. Catherine's therapy has actually spiced things up a bit. Maybe you two should try it.

Yeah, right. Peter's a professional but he'd rather lose a limb than go to couple's therapy.

At that moment, Catherine walked up behind Marina and wrapped her glistening, sweaty arms around her. She smiled coyly, suggesting she'd overheard them, her face splotched red.

Yuck! Catherine! Marina said in mock annoyance, squirming out of her grip. You're soaking and disgusting. And now so am I.

How was your run? Alice asked, looking up, her hand in a lazy salute to keep the sun from blinding her.

Great run. I'm jumping in the ocean to cool off, and then I'll get dinner rounded up. I'm starving! Come swim with me, Marina. Now that you're as sweaty as I am, she said, dragging her wife toward the beach.

Peter stood under the water in the outdoor shower much longer than necessary; hot water meditation. No phone. No Alice. No hostesses. Dressing as he stared out at the waves breaking not fifty feet from the window, he wondered what to plan for the next day. Alice, Marina, and Catherine would go to the beach and then almost certainly go shopping in East Hampton. The only thing that interested him downtown was BookHampton. He did need something new to read, having abandoned the much-lauded Jill Lepore *These Truths*. Thinking about the Constitution made him ill.

A half hour later he was dressed in shorts and one of his new Lorenzini shirts. Ready to face the women. Did they keep gin in the house—or should he stick to wine? He'd been drinking too much lately, but an icy martini would be perfection. Of course they kept a full bar! Staring at the array of clear and amber liquids in the heavy glass bottles arrayed on the bar cart he zeroed in on the gin. Hendrick's would do.

Emerging from the house, the sexy little martini glass in hand, he observed that the women were well into the wine. The martini would catch him right up. Settling into a massive teak armchair, he reflected on his good fortune. Alice was looking very pretty in white linen, the soft yellow-orange light of the setting sun coming through her long hair. He thought of taking her picture but he had a strict no sunset policy, and there was no way to get Alice without the fiery scene unfolding behind her.

You're all looking very beautiful, he said.

Well thank you, Peter. You look quite sharp yourself. I like that shirt, Catherine said.

It is nice, Alice said. The pink suits you. Have you decided to go preppy on me?

Yes, Alice. Don't you see the little whale? And the tiny whales on my shorts? I may have one on my boxers—but you'll have to discover it for yourself.

Can't wait, she said a little too drily. Peter had never owned a single item of clothing with a critter of any sort stitched on it—nary a whale, polo pony, or alligator. The pink shirt's feminine flair was more interesting than his ordinary blues and whites. He was a handsome man, if she could manage to see it.

How's work? Marina asked, looking at Peter.

Work? Work is busy. I can't seem to graduate my patients. They just keep coming back.

Oh, did no one tell you your patients never leave? They're like characters in my novels. They never seem to know when it's time to exit left. Always begging for sequels, said Marina.

Did you know I've been seeing someone? Catherine chimed in. A woman on the Upper West Side, not far, really, from your office.

What's the name? If you don't mind me asking.

Dr. Daniella Weiss. She's on 83rd and Amsterdam. I got her name from Sally. I suppose I should have asked you. Have you heard of her?

I have. Small world. Dr. Weiss and I were on a panel together three or four years ago. *Reconsidering Twenty-First-Century Psychoanalytic Practices: The Rise/Demise of the Symbolic and Pragmatic Function of the Recumbent Position.* Title was too clever by half but I didn't write it.

Care to translate? What the hell was the panel about? Marina asked.

What, it's not clear? The couch! Of course. Peter could feel the very edges of the martini softening his thoughts, infusing the view and the conversation with pleasure. The day was falling away as his wound-up thoughts gave in to the effects of the alcohol without blurring them.

What is your position on the couch, if you'll forgive the pun? Catherine asked. Dr. Weiss and I discussed analysis and the use of the couch. I may consider it in the fall when we're back in New York full-time. I know it's terribly unsophisticated of me, but I can't see using the couch.

What sort of couch does Dr. Weiss have?

You're asking the right girl, Peter. Who loves furniture more than I do? The thing is a bit of a travesty. Let's just say it's an exotically feminine fuchsia linen recamier. An Annie Selke. Even if it isn't tasteful—or maybe because it's not—lying down on it would be an invitation to seduction.

Well, well, Catherine. Happy to hear the transference is coming along nicely, Peter said.

Really, Peter. What's the point? Catherine asked.

The point, said Alice, jumping in, is that you're staring at the clock, not at the doctor, and she's free to check her phone.

Hardly, Alice, said Peter with annoyance. I'm sure you'd agree it's a useful tool, the line of sight is just one tiny benefit. Turning his eyes to Catherine, he went on: The transgressive potential of recumbence is what you're articulating. And you're not wrong. The combination of intimacy and distancing the position offers is no accident. It's a vestige of Freud, who was steeped in the language and material culture of the rest cure— the sanatorium. Think of *The Magic Mountain*.

The what?

It's a very long novel by Thomas Mann, Alice said.

Oh sorry. Catherine looked mildly embarrassed. Alice thought Peter was showing off. He should have known she wasn't a reader.

Not at all, Peter said quickly. Nobody reads that book anymore. Anyway, Freud would have associated healing, rest, and comfort. Early in his career he dallied in hypnosis, which required the patient to be recumbent. The bed-like divan or chaise or couch—whatever you want to call it—evolved out of a broader tradition of healing involving hydrotherapy, rest cures, massage, brushing. The talking cure won the beauty contest.

So do your patients use the couch? And what does yours look like? Marina asked.

Oh, Peter is quite proud of his couch. He discovered it at an antique store on East 98th Street back in the eighties. It was a birthday gift from his mother—

Not just my mother, Alice. From both parents. It's quite simple, really. Tufted green velvet. I am proud of it. Alice is right. Really, though, the thing is a negation of Freud's orientalist aesthetic. His Turkish divan was the centerpiece of an antique office filled with cigar smoke, kilims, and other rich fabric.

Sounds plush and sexy to me, Marina said. And what is the analyst's office if not a scene of seduction?

Let's hope not literally, Peter replied with an awkward laugh. The truth is, the couch is an icon of the profession. It's not a particularly functional piece of furniture anymore. Last patient who actually used mine had a broken leg. But any self-respecting analyst wouldn't be without one.

Peter's full thoughts about the couch weren't put into words. He admired and feared the sensuous traditions the couch embodied, with its history of supine women in their own zone of privacy. Images of reclining figures crowded his mind—Renoir's *Large Nude*, Giorgione's *The Sleeping Venus*, Titian's *Venus of Urbino*, Manet's *Olympia*, and his favorite, Casas i Carbo's *After the Ball*, in which the figure's soft body—flopped on the sofa in her black ball gown, book in hand—stands in contrast with an expression of boredom mixed with rage on the woman's gentle face. Recumbent speech suggested an ambiguous, troubling history of eroticism, with the cheap phrase *pillow talk* leaving untouched the genuine intimacy such speech invited.

Friday, August 17

The defining scent of August in Manhattan registers canine and human waste. After weeks without rain, the greasy sidewalks exuded a nauseating olfactory complexity; Alice identified it as the ripe scent of an unwashed human body dominated by the rich gases put off by a substratum of gram-negative bacteria. Stepping into the underworld at 72nd Street with her Citarella grocery bag, Alice swiped her fare just in time to rush into a surprisingly empty car. As the doors closed behind her the oppressive heat and humidity were nothing next to the regret of having been tricked.

If Alice stepped into one more hot car on the 1, 2, 3 line, she swore she'd give up the damn subway. As she sweated in the sticky air, she decided the dilemma of the hot car presented a clumsy metaphor for life. The car attracts because it's empty, as if nobody else on the crowded platforms up and down the island has noticed this attractive option with its free seats and room to move. *Stand clear of the closing doors.* Once the doors close, the recognition of choosing poorly becomes a question of action or inaction: move cars or enjoy the rare opportunity

to sit down on one of the many free seats? Most people chose
to move. Peter did every time, raging at the MTA and Cuomo
and the ineffectual ass of a mayor he'd voted for while stepping onto the platform at the next stop and then back onto the
train again in the closest car. Some people, without so much as
sitting down, took the panhandler's escape: a walk on the shaking metal bridge suspended between cars as the train passed
through the dark, sultry tunnel at twenty miles per hour. But
there were always a few defeated bodies who stayed put, suc-
cumbing to their mistake.

The broken air-conditioning units on subways proliferated
as the summer progressed—overworked and undermaintained,
the heat won. Come August, with mechanics on vacation and air
conditioners taxed to exhaustion, many New Yorkers submitted,
damp and defeated, to the expanding backlog of hot cars awaiting repair. It was as if the heat of the warming atmosphere had
triumphed, or maybe, thought Alice, the hot cars were a warning
of what the subway would feel like when humanity recognized
that the luxury of cooling—*conditioning*—the air was suicidal.
A three-inch rise in sea level by 2040? She might as well get
used to the hot car, or at least feel fleetingly good about the status it conferred on her as a non-contributor to the impending
catastrophe. As the train approached 79th Street, Alice's first
easy opportunity to change cars, she remained seated, her white
cotton blouse growing damp as her body worked inefficiently
to cool itself. What did it matter?

Placing his bottle of Barr Hill Gin on the counter, Peter prepped
his martini glass by filling it with ice water. It wasn't every night

that he indulged in what was essentially an elegant tranquil-
izer, but he needed it. Besides, it was Friday, the first day of his
two-week August vacation. What a fine feeling: all that time
wide open before him with nothing but a short review to finish
for the *International Journal of Psychoanalysis*, the arrival of the
girls, and Labor Day at the Donnes. Neatly settling the snug
cap on the stainless steel shaker, he shook the canister forcefully, the sound briefly deafening. In his mind, the noise was
tiny shards of ice shearing off the cubes as they repeatedly hit
against the sides of the metal shaker. The goal was booze so
cold that if it had been water it would have been slush. Then
his phone vibrated.

Alice took a sip of wine as she watched him set the
shaker on the counter and reach for the device, turning the face
toward him to see who was calling. He looked briefly perplexed
and then slid his thumb over the screen's face to accept.
Lisbeth. It's nice you called.

Alice gazed at him, unconsciously raising a single eyebrow and trying to catch his eye. He was entirely absorbed.
Somewhere between mocking and ironic, her stance at the
moment was one of humored skepticism. His voice sounded
oddly syrupy—kind, with a quality of softness that reminded
Alice of the whisper one invokes when trying not to frighten a
lost child or small animal. But there was something else in his
voice, something unfamiliar. Was it nerves? Before Alice could
decide, Peter had slipped down the hallway to his office. Alice
heard the decisive click of the door closing him in. She poured
herself another glass of the excellent South African chenin
blanc. She wouldn't have minded overhearing his conversation, but the hall was silent—even when she padded barefoot

carefully down it and stood, as casually as she could, pretending to look for something in the closet just outside his office door.

It was thrilling and dangerous to have Lisbeth's voice with him as he stood there, surrounded by his things, in the space where he'd thought of her much too often. The act of the phone call brought her closer, testifying to his importance in her life and underlining a bond between them that now went beyond the confines of his office. She was different—special. Not like other patients. And she trusted him. As she described the miseries of her day, he lowered himself into his overstuffed chair, immediately recognizing the familiar stirring in his groin. He was already hard by the time he realized how wrong it was. Before he could think about how much he didn't want to go down this dark moral pathway, he'd unzipped. It was wrong—but whom did it harm? Imagining her lying nude on the bed in her West Village apartment, he absorbed her voice more than her words. She wasn't crying. She was missing him or, more precisely, anticipating missing him. It only took a moment.

Twenty-five minutes later he went to the bathroom, flushed the tissue, splashed his face with water, and examined his appearance. Nothing telling. Invigorated, Peter felt more alive than he had in months—no, years. Now he really was ready for that martini. But what the hell did it mean? He knew he was in trouble—the ethics of jerking off while on the phone with a patient were murky, but not all that murky. If only he were still Catholic, but he'd quit the church at the age of eleven. Eliciting the feeling of confession as a boy, the darkness, the kneeling down in the close room, the mysterious sound of the priest's movements, a faint rustling on the other side of the wall, and then the dread of speaking overcome by the miracle of confession. *I lied to my mother, my teacher, my sister. I swore. I had impure thoughts.* There it was—impure thoughts. That was one way to put it. Ah, to expiate himself fully. What a relief it would be to rid himself of the sordid secret of his act—this one and the one in his office. Only moments had passed since he'd had her voice in his ear, but the regret and shame had already obliterated his exhilaration. A lot of good Dr. March had done him. He couldn't think of anybody else to talk to.

Scrambling to rationalize, he told himself that the event was no more than an extension of what counted as Peter's sex life. In fact, it was a considerable step up from the anonymous stimulation he'd grown used to. His first experiment with online porn was so long ago that the modem had announced his activity with that now impossibly antique dial-up noise, the beeps, twangs, and clicks fraught with potential failure. He'd been at his desk, Alice and the girls—still just babies—at the grocery store. As vaguely degrading as it had felt to watch the action of excruciatingly pixilated sexual parts in action, jerking off to the videos came uncomfortably close to fucking a stranger. The medium contained a wonderland of sexual possibility. He'd returned often, each time as grateful to technology, liberal values, and the internet as he was happily astonished at the possibilities.

His persistent fantasies about the sexual acts of strangers had long since altered his relationship with Alice. Even if getting off on porn wasn't cheating, by engaging in it as often as he did he found himself in a private sexual landscape, one that didn't include her, her body, or even the kinds of sexual acts they had once engaged in together. Peter liked to think Alice was as satisfied with her virtual sex life as he was with his. As far as he was concerned, porn had liberated them both from the necessity of the other's body and the outlandish presumption that one other body could—or should—fulfill each of their sexual needs until death. If something called intimacy was a casualty, so be it.

Hell, he figured, maybe they wouldn't have made it as far as they had without their rich fantasy lives juiced by moving images to fill the physical gap now most starkly represented by the furniture—separate beds implemented under the guise of snoring and divergent sleep schedules. Peter felt no need to justify his porn habit. The marital familiarity souring to boredom and, most of all, her sexual reluctance amounted to permission to do as he pleased. Why was she so hard and closed to him, anyway? True, she couldn't compete with the effortless availability, youth, naughtiness, and delicious variety of screen images. She couldn't and she hadn't tried. But she didn't have to. He didn't need youth—however much he lusted after it. He simply wanted to be desired.

Peter emerged from his office, his face flushed. She'd heard the toilet flush, but before that he'd been in his office forever. Half an hour at least. Alice had put some eggs on the stove—it was a night for croque madames. A simple dinner. But his long absence was more than strange. Alice sensed something amiss, but what? Was Lisbeth a colleague or a patient? She didn't know Dr. Peak's first name, the woman who shared his office suite. She'd called before. Maybe she was having problems again. The woman was a terrible psychiatrist: cold, impatient, and imperious. She had few patients. Peter had referred one or two people to her when he couldn't fit them into his schedule, but they'd later complained about her manner and moved on, seeking solace, advice, meds, and warmth in their lives from other sources.

Who was that?

Just a patient.

Just a patient? Alice repeated archly, raising that eyebrow again. She waited for his answer, watching him, the trim khakis and ordinary dress shirt representative of his return to tiresome conservatism in clothing. How did men get away with such mundane presentations of their physical selves? He repulsed her with his sneaky phone call and pretense of normalcy as he swirled the silent shaker containing his ruined martini. The clank of ice absent, he placed it back on the counter, defeated, the shaker so warm it had ceased sweating.

Yes. She's quite volatile, and I offered her my number to prevent something worse than her bothering me after hours from happening.

You said you'd never do that is all. I'm a bit surprised. I don't care, really. Just surprised. Alice could feel her voice tightening. What a fucking hypocrite he was. *Quite volatile*. Please.

Peter had offered Lisbeth his private number just that day, with instruction to call or text if she was feeling particularly down. It was the sort of boundary he didn't like to cross. It invited too much identification in the patient, the calls and texts simulating an invitation into his private existence that was potentially damaging to the patient's autonomy. Phone calls after hours were a slippery slope—as he'd just demonstrated. In Lisbeth's case he'd told himself he needed to balance his policy against his fear that she would harm herself over the two weeks he was out of the office. The truth of it, as he could see most clearly only after her phone call, was that he'd given her his number not because she needed it but because he liked the idea of engaging with her outside the rigid confines of The

Hour. But what was he going to say to Alice? He was afraid she could see the truth—that he'd left some sign on his face or body that would give away his sordid doings.

It's really not unusual. There's nothing wrong with it. Many of my colleagues give out home numbers and invite patients to call. It's judgment. Some cases demand extra effort. The literature agrees—

We're not talking about the literature, are we? We're talking about you. And I don't know why you're suddenly so defensive. Like I said. I don't care. So, who is she?

You know I can't talk about my patients—

That's a laugh, Alice snorted, interrupting him. Since when? Since the dinner at the Meyers' when you went on about that Wall Street guy, or since you asked me what I thought of that depressive drinking too much wine and popping Valium, or since you would not shut up about that hypercritical woman who refused to pay her bill. Since when is it, exactly, that you don't talk about your patients?

Give me a fucking break. Jesus!

He'd screwed up. But he wasn't about to give Alice the right to tell him how to run his practice. What the hell did she know about it?

Fine. Never mind. I just know you don't believe in it. That's all. So why—

Leave it, Alice. Just leave it. He turned, dumping the watery gin down the sink. So much for the pleasant afterglow.

I am not a dog dropping a stick. If there's any fetching and dropping to be done here it's not going to be by me, she said to his back, her face growing hot as she attempted to contain her temper. She wasn't at all sure what she meant by this nonsense, having gotten carried away by the metaphor and her burgeoning sense of outrage. But what did it matter? Things were getting heated without much cause.

Did I say that? You know, Alice, you've been acting strange. Let's talk about you. What's going on? Why don't we talk about why you stopped looking for Maebelle and decided instead to roam around the apartment for the past two months, your earbuds in like a goddamn sixteen-year-old girl.

Oh, you're interested in talking? Excellent, Peter. That's just excellent. Because it comes as a giant fucking surprise to me. I can't remember the last time you spoke to me for more than five minutes. And you wonder why I'm curious which of your patients could possibly hold your attention on the phone for half an hour?

You're jealous? Really? You know, Alice, I'd like to have something to say to you. I really would. Maybe if you weren't quite so small.

At this, Alice was at a loss for words. She wanted—no, needed—to inflict major damage because she feared that she was in fact small, a tad mean, and definitely selfish. Too self-contained. All of the truth of being small—and that cruel expression—made the accusation disproportionately painful and impossible to let go. *Fuck you* or *you're an asshole* would not do. The force of these insults and most others like them had long since been depleted by overuse. A long marriage could do that, even to a rich vocabulary.

Small? Really?

From the depths of her rage, unhinged and desperate to strike back, she surprised herself by picking up an empty glass from the counter and throwing it across the kitchen at

Peter. Acting quickly, she didn't have time to consider what she was doing. She knew it was radical, but beyond that she didn't think. She was furious, and the glass was there. Seeing it prompted an irresistible impulse to throw the object at Peter, whom she hated at that moment more than she hated anyone or anything in the world. Never having had much of an arm, she didn't consider the possibility that the missive would hit the mark. It wasn't dangerous. She threw to hear it shatter, to feel the freedom and rush of the unreasonable act.

One moment it was in the air and the next he went at her with a fury more surprising than anything in their twenty-two-year marriage. His fists pounding on her back, she curled in by rounding her shoulders and gripping her head with her hands to protect it. He came at her with all that masculine strength—a strength that will almost always take a woman by surprise no matter how tall or strong she might be. Off her guard at the bizarre turn of events, Alice at first simply protected herself, but when he paused she turned instinctively to push him back, kicking toward him in wide swaths to keep him as far from her as possible.

Fear had rushed upon her, forceful and surprising, but it wasn't long before he reignited her rage. That was when she threw the second glass at him. And the third. They were wonderfully effective at keeping him off balance. Grasping a fine green and then a blue tumbler, winding up and letting them loose in the air conferred an unfamiliar freedom. Throwing them was reckless and violent in a way that suited Alice's sense of the world out of order.

Without another in reach, Peter took his moment to come back on the attack, this time grabbing the handle of the pan containing the two sunny-side-up eggs she'd been frying in olive oil. As if the pan were a tennis racket and the eggs balls he was returning, he aimed them at her head. Alice ducked, the hot mess mostly passing into the air to the side of her face. The fragrant olive oil, already hot enough to solidify the edge of the albumen, grazed her cheek while the eggs continued their unlikely journey through the air. Yolk and slimy white mixed with shreds of cooked egg plastered the face of the refrigerator and the coffee machine, and then dripped down between the peanuts, almonds, and Brazil nuts in a bowl on the counter. It was as if Peter's rage had materialized, exploding as a semi-liquid mess.

As the pan clattered to the floor, the chaos of the fight was on with renewed fury. What was happening felt dangerous to both of them. It had gone too far. What was next? Each was aware that the other might grab a knife, knock a head against a counter, or land a violent blow that would do real damage. Alice began kicking at Peter again, both to protect herself and because she wanted to hurt him. But with nothing to throw she was left with her weak fists and feet. As much as she wanted to do him harm, she didn't have the skills or strength.

As abruptly as Alice had started it, they were done. Movement stopped: which one of them let up first she never knew. They backed gingerly away from each another, as one might from a sleeping infant, moving as slowly and carefully as possible. After a brief silence, ugly things were said about divorce. Alice told Peter she hated him. Peter told Alice he hated her.

It was at that moment that she realized the first glass she'd thrown had cut Peter's face, a reality she'd missed in the rush of her radical action. Diagonal to the narrow line of hair that formed his eyebrow was a slim gash. With each pump of his heart, tiny drops of blood fell onto his blue-and-white-striped dress shirt. Then Alice understood. Peter's astonishing rage at the onset was a visceral reaction to pain.

I'm not proud I hit you. I'm sorry. But if you ever use it against me, things will be bad for you.

What the fuck? You're the one with the big cut, the big bloody evidence right there on your face, she said. How like him to think of what the world thought—that she would somehow use the kicking and hitting against him. Did he fear she'd tell somebody, or was he already in divorce court? Did he think she'd tell the police? Hardly. She'd started it, for Christ's sake.

Peter began to clean, an action that calmed him at the best of times and now felt like the only way to ground himself, the only way to make sense of the line that had just been crossed. Alice fled, shaking and crying and shimmering with olive oil. In her room she curled up on her bed and wept, rage and regret fueling the tears. It felt like the end—but how could it be? It had all happened too fast. An anomaly, the fury of the physical fight so out of keeping with their normally civilized rage, a rage that simmered beneath the surface of every word and action when they were together, a rage that was safe and comfortable and familiar. It was a thing they'd both agreed to contain, a feral animal they'd consented to keep but lock up for everyone's good. Now it was out.

Horribly alone in the quiet of her room, she could hear him in the kitchen. The sound of glass rang through the air, the shards scraping against the metal dustpan as he swept the menacing blue and green chunks and splinters together into a neat pile. Alice divined their curious authority, the translucent pieces painted with dandelion-yellow yolk. All that glass—she wanted to take it to her bed and run it over her skin until the blood came. She would be cleansed.

He worked for half an hour, and then the apartment went quiet. He knocked at her door. Standing to meet him in the neutral territory of the hall, she spoke first.

I'm sorry I cut your face. I didn't mean to. He looked up with the green-and-yellow sponge still in his hand.

I'm sorry, too.

And then they laughed uneasily and hugged and joked about how impressive it had been—and fun! Just to fucking lose it. To throw shit and scream and beat on each other with their bare hands. It was more cathartic than sex. More vital and infinitely sexier than their sex had been for a long time.

Tenderly, he took her chin in his hand, turning her face to see her cheek where the hot oil had made contact with her skin. There on her right cheek was a bright red area that might have been sunburned or chapped. Nothing more.

I'm sorry. I could have really hurt you. You're sure you're okay? I didn't realize it was so hot.

It's nothing. I'm fine.

They stepped into the bathroom together where she dabbed his cut with a damp towel and carefully placed a Band-Aid over the gash. It looked quite silly—the Band-Aid there on his face right above his eye.

You should get a stitch.

She said it knowing that he wanted her to suggest he go to the emergency room even though she didn't think he needed to. It was deep, but it would heal. What it really needed was one of those antiquated butterfly bandages. But there weren't any in the medicine cabinet, and Peter demurred when Alice offered to go buy a box.

No. It'll be fine. I'll think about it later.

He spoke a little coldly then, and Alice felt the damage they'd done, the distance they'd created between themselves. Alice regretted it wasn't her with the cut above her eye. She felt like a brute; he was the victim, no matter her rosy cheek and tiny bruises. They'd have to invent a fiction for the girls to explain away Peter's scar. It was easily done.

Peter dropped onto his bed, slaughtered by the adrenalin-dopamine tsunami of orgasm, fight, and wound. His cut throbbed, telling him more than he wanted to know about his heart's pace. The Lisinopril didn't have a chance against a heart working as hard as his. Flat on his back he stared at the blank, chalky ceiling. Alice was doing god-knows-what somewhere else, and good riddance to her. Did she act as if she were superior, or was he simply sodden with guilt? He reflected on his mistakes. He'd hit Alice. That was unforgivable even if she'd hurt him with that glass—and cut open his face. Then there was the fresh memory of what a pig he'd been. There was no dodging that. But he'd do it again—which made him even more of a pig. Regret of the sort that he could have put to use was nowhere available. Did he wish he didn't want to fuck Lisbeth? Certainly. But that third-order desire was academic. He did want to. Very much. Right at that moment more than ever.

Monday, August 27,
and Thursday,
August 30

A deep sense of abandon, of not giving a fuck if his life went to hell before the summer ended and he was forced to clean it all up—or not—had Peter watching porn and jerking off more than usual, often waiting out his refractory period with a brief nap before having another go. Alice's responses to the tension between them and the stress of his constant presence in the apartment were comparatively simple and wholesome: she'd been working incessantly, eating too much heavily buttered toast, and drinking more wine than was strictly acceptable starting at 5 PM—or a hair prior. Pretending it was less than a bottle wasn't a game she could sportingly play with herself anymore. So she didn't.

She'd begun to loathe summer. As it wound down, no matter how conscious they might be of the question's stupidity, nobody was able to stop themselves from asking, *How was your summer?* It was as if everyone she knew had agreed it was suddenly acceptable to go around talking about the weather. The answers, no less than the question, were pointedly banal.

Fine. Hot.

Ready for it to be over.

Terrific, yours?

Best ever.

Highs and lows.

Alice had recently encountered one of the women from the lost dog association in the freezer aisle at Fairway. As she recalled, she'd been the one sporting pink frosted toe polish, but Alice was not attuned to faces so she couldn't be sure. And never mind the name; that was hopeless. She hadn't been in touch with any of them since that first meeting, although she knew the meetings had continued. It all seemed very long ago.

Oh! Alice, isn't it? What are you up to?

Um, just in here looking for something for dinner.

Really? Haven't seen you in so long. How's your summer?

Busy! Alice said, turning away to reach for a bag of frozen peas.

After that, Alice decided to say *tragic* rather than *busy* the next time someone asked her how her fucking summer was.

Alice walked toward home with the groceries for the girls, who would be arriving the next day. She looked forward to indulging them before they all left for the Berkshires by buying the foods she knew they would both want and allow themselves to eat: precious clamshells of fresh blueberries, blackberries, and raspberries, airy ginger-peach frozen yogurt, grainy bread from the bakery upstate. For dinner she would relish roasting a big chicken stuffed with herbs—for them.

Turning the corner from Broadway onto 96th Street, Alice eyed a particularly busy pile of boxes, blankets, and plastic bags tucked into a defunct entryway of a former CVS. At first glance, she couldn't even see a human body, but what she did spot was what appeared to be an empty Cup Noodles filled with water. How many times, she wondered, as she peered at the slow rise and fall of the blankets, would she get her hopes up? When would she stop looking? Alice set her groceries down and carefully approached the Dunkin' Donuts begging cup. The flap of a packing box flat on the sidewalk in front of the cup had been decorated with a heart and block letters that read: ANYTHING HELPS. HUNGRY. NEED BUS FARE. GOD BLESS. Alice stared, perplexed. The water bowl, if that's what it was, might indicate nonhuman life. As she stood rudely staring, the corner of the blanket rose slightly. Alice prepared herself, expecting she'd soon be engaged with a disheveled figure appearing from under the blanket, but instead what emerged was a deeply familiar black nose followed immediately by the most lovable face in her world: Maebelle.

As instinctively as she'd pulled her children back from a car backing up in a parking lot, Alice decisively grabbed her dog. By the time she had her in her arms, Maebelle was emitting a high-pitched bark-whine that Alice well knew from the many times she'd returned from a trip. It was a cry of crazed joy accompanied by an explosion of movement. Tuning herself up into a higher key, the little dog squirmed in her arms, propelling herself as best she could toward Alice's face where her tiny tongue sought skin to lick in an action that surely approximated kissing.

Time had slowed, the moments between seeing the water bowl and the present imprinted themselves on her mind in granular physicality. Suddenly afraid of a confrontation,

Alice turned and walked rapidly down the block toward her apartment as fast as she could without drawing attention to herself. As soon as she was beyond reach of Maebelle's former encampment, she broke into a run, the little dog bouncing up and down in her arms as she made her way west toward the river, toward home. The raw chicken, bread, expensive berries, and soon-to-be-liquid frozen yogurt remained behind on the sidewalk.

Back in the empty apartment, Alice set Maebelle on her lap and, with her tiny face in her hands, told her how much she had missed her, what a naughty girl she'd been to run away, how she forgave her and loved her. Peter had gone to a movie. She wanted him home. She needed to share her joy, to make it real by telling him. Never mind, she thought. I'll surprise him. Teary, messy, and overjoyed, Alice tried to compute the reality of having Maebelle back. Rubbing her belly, she recognized that she'd intellectually but not emotionally given up on finding her. She hadn't fully mourned her loss. She'd been waiting. Still waiting. And now she felt fresh and happy as a girl.

After feeding her kibble from the bag she hadn't been able to throw out, she put Maebelle in the tub. To wash away the stranger who'd kept her as much as the scent of the street, she held the water-averse animal under the steady stream, soaking the fur before sudsing her into a rich lather with a dab of her thirty-dollar Pureology keratin color-safe shampoo. Maebelle, looking more rat than dog, was then rinsed and swaddled in a fresh white towel, at which point she calmed, the papoose rendering her cozy as an infant. Holding the weight of the dog in her arms, Alice's world was complete. Gazing at the adorable bundle, she experienced an extraordinary lightness, as if nothing mattered but the presence of herself and her dog in the pretty room with the light filtering through the leaves of her plants.

Balthazar was a family favorite even if it had priced itself out of any real relation to its value. Worse, it had become a tourist mecca—listed in *Time Out New York* as *a must-go Soho bistro scene* and in *Fodor's as the Paris bistro you'll find only in New York City*. The tourists detracted from the experience but couldn't ruin it. Birthdays and graduation meals had been eaten there—with many golden-hued photos to document the excesses of Chablis, seafood towers, garlicky escargot, vegetable terrines, Côtes du Rhône, steak tartar, béarnaise and frites, profiteroles and crème brûlée. For once it was possible to reserve a table for four at 8 PM without planning two months in advance. One of the scarce virtues of August in the city.

To have her girls back was all Alice needed to complete her happiness. She'd put fresh sheets on their beds, which were now together in one room, cleaned the bathrooms, set out towels, and returned to Fairway to replace the lost groceries.

When they'd arrived, the air had been fragrant with roast chicken and thyme. After she hugged them too tightly on arrival, she couldn't stop herself from repeating the action twice over the course of the evening, practically sneaking up on them from behind and wrapping her arms around them. They returned her affection, and yet they were more self-contained than she wanted them to be. Never mind, she told herself. It felt so good to enclose their familiar bodies with hers, to have them safe and near, to smell and see the changes, to admire the clothes she'd never seen, never mind not shopped with them for, and to wonder at the sophistication of the work they described doing over the summer months.

Looking at them now across the white tablecloth at Balthazar, amid the riot of glasses, plates, bottles, and silverware, Alice was strangely concerned to see the California freshness and understated glamour that had attached itself to them over the course of the spring and summer. It had been, incredibly, almost five months since Easter break when she'd last seen them. As the waiter refilled their glasses in the din of the busy restaurant, she realized she didn't want them to be too attractive. How misleading that prize could be, drawing all sorts of unworthy admirers and filling their heads with mistaken ideas about value. It was better to be plain, forced to rely on wits and hard work rather than the easy exchange of social capital that had not been honestly come by. A plain woman wasn't easily swept off course. But there was nothing to be done about it; both of them were stunning. What could she do but bask in the glow of their beauty and the vitality of the unexpected changes?

Once they'd ordered, Alice retold the shocking story of Maebelle while Peter editorialized about how obsessed Alice had been all summer. The lost-and-found dog story had already become a practiced anecdote.

I was so happy to have her back, Alice explained, that it wasn't until the next morning that it occurred to me to thank the person who had kept her all that time.

Wait, you really never talked to her? You hadn't thanked her? asked Bette.

No, in the moment I had to take her. I was afraid to have a fight, so I just ran. I went back the next morning—

Without Maebelle, Peter added.

Yes, continued Alice. I went back hoping the person would still be there. I never even really saw anyone, or if I did I had no recollection of them. The pile of stuff was still there but whomever it was remained under the blanket. How do you knock on a blanket? I just said, *Hello, hello*. The blanket moved a little and then out came a grimy hand followed by a girl a little older than you two with blonde dreadlocks. Her dirty skin was hardly covered by a tiny camisole and jean shorts. *What?* she said—and not in a friendly way. She was tough. I said, *I found my dog yesterday, and I think you took care of her. I wanted to thank you.* I was pretty nervous. I mean, what if she accused me of stealing her dog? Sure enough, she said, *So you're the bitch who stole my dog.* With that, she stood up and came right up to me. I was afraid she was going to grab hold of me but I stood my ground. She said, *I want Lucy back. She's mine.* I then stupidly—I mean, what did it matter—told her that her name was Maebelle and that she had been lost just before Memorial Day. I told her I'd been looking for her all summer. Then I said I was sorry for the fifth time. Could I do anything for her? *I'd like to give you some money, in thanks.* She said, *Put it in the cup.* So I stuffed this wad of bills into her Dunkin' Donuts cup. She didn't even look at it. She just turned her back with a loud *Fuck off*. It was not the most satisfying philanthropic experience of my life. I'm so grateful to her. I'd do more if I could.

Wait, Mom. How much money did you give her? Emile asked.

Enough.

Wasn't the reward two thousand?

Well, yes, but . . . Alice looked at Peter, who locked eyes with her while raising his eyebrows.

She didn't exactly return her, he said. I mean, you could argue your mom is the one who found her. Maybe we should give her the reward.

Mom. You should give her the reward, Bette said. I mean, she kept her safe all that time.

You're right, I'm sure, Alice said quietly as Peter jumped in.

Maybe if she hadn't had her, someone who actually paid attention to the world around them would have returned her that same day rather than keeping her for three months. Three months she had her! You could even argue she stole her. And you think we should give her the reward?

Dad! Both girls said in unison.

It's not as if she gave the dog back, and besides, technically the reward was no longer being offered. The flyers were all taken down weeks ago, Peter replied.

Yeah, like that matters, Dad, Emile said.

Alice remained quiet. She had given the girl the full reward: $2,000. But she didn't want to advertise the fact—she didn't want Peter to accuse her of wasting what was essentially his hard-earned money. Even more important to her though was holding on to the knowledge of what she saw as her goodness. She wanted the kindness and generosity of her impulse to be sacrosanct. Telling anyone—even the girls—that she'd done it would compromise her gesture, as if she'd done it to be admired. But now it had gotten all twisted around, and she was being accused of being stingy.

Smoked trout salad, the waiter said, placing the plate in front of Alice. The girls' escargot landed and Peter's appetizer portion of steak tartar. Taking up his fork, he tucked the prongs under the raw meat on his plate, his mouth watering in anticipation of the first rich, savory bite. He'd be damned if he was giving up two grand. How, he wondered as he bit down on a caper, had he raised such sanctimonious kids? They'd never really had to work to support themselves. Maybe that was part of it.

Bette and Emile exchanged glances but did not take up the subject again. They ate in silence for a moment, each one cooling with their own thoughts as they dipped bread in the scalding garlicky butter surrounding the oversize snail shells, containing the tiny, chewy mollusks.

To any observer they appeared to be the ideal family: they handled their silverware with enviable grace, they dabbed their starched napkins at their mouths, they sipped their wine and delicately tore their bread. From their cheekbones to their cuticles they were well-groomed; their clothes were modest and nicely fitted, dominated by earth tones that bespoke taste and restraint. Nobody, not counting Alice's stacked gold rings, wore too much jewelry. You would have been hard-pressed to identify makeup on any of them. But then, almost everyone in the restaurant looked tasteful and prosperous. It was the soft, yellow light that did it. The place was teeming with gorgeous, happy people.

Peter, wearing one of his new shirts, had whitened his teeth. How relieved he was Alice hadn't said anything. Had she noticed? Did he hope Lisbeth's subconscious would absorb the effect when he returned in September? She'd called frequently over the past ten days, always late in the afternoon. She'd intuited that calling at this hour would give her a more

intact, complete version of Peter—the Dr. Nutting she longed
for from session. She'd been forced to leave several messages
that Peter hastily deleted—but he could still listen to them
again and again as deleted voicemails remained accessible but
invisible to Alice were she to happen to get hold of his phone.

He had no idea what to do about his distressing lust for
the girl. And now, the proximity of his own daughters—not
much younger than Lisbeth—their immediate presences, left
him with a queasy gut. His malevolent behavior had grown
so ordinary. He knew he should resolve the problem before
sessions began again in September. Was he even capable of
restraint, or was the whole thing heading toward a ruinous
physical expression? That fucking avalanche unleashing in
whatever crazy chaos Dr. March had gone on about? Maybe
the male instinct to fuck and fuck young couldn't be avoided.
He was weary of living with the fear of discovery but equally
sick of porn without a tenable, warm object. He didn't think
Lisbeth knew what he'd been up to on the other end of the
line—but he couldn't be sure. Surely, she lacked proof. But if
that had ever mattered, it didn't anymore. The whisper of an
accusation would ruin him.

And what about Alice? It was as if she knew and had
decided that it didn't matter to her. She'd never again asked
about Lisbeth or the phone calls. Her silence disconcerted him.
If she knew or suspected something he'd had no fresh hint of
it. Was she enjoying observing his demise, standing virtuously
to the side while he imploded? She'd been so preoccupied,
passing endless hours in her office, door closed. And now that
she had Maebelle back, she needed him even less—if that were
possible. She certainly wasn't going to confront him, and in

the absence of any external source of accountability he'd failed to evolve beyond his feeble initial instinct that he was doing something wrong while continuing to do it all the same. Each time Lisbeth called he experienced a flash of justification: he was helping her, and maybe there was nothing so wrong with his fantasy. For that was all it really was: a fantasy mixed with a bit of harmless physical pleasure. At least for now.

Saturday–Monday,
September 1–3,
Labor Day Weekend

The lemony goldenrod and gaudy purple vetch turned the country painterly. Trespassing with enviable abandon, the colors splattered backyards, fields, medians, and roadsides. Equally ruthless and efficient, pokeweed appeared out of place, towering over the restrained politeness of the native undergrowth with rows of jammy berries, juicy central stalks, and elephantine leaves. On the skyline, the maple and poplar trees threatened to give up their relentlessly monochromatic verdure but as yet showed no real sign of retreat, while the birch leaves made them appear plain by shimmering silver in the breeze.

The rest of the guests had arrived at the Donnes' the night before. As a group they were fatter and tanner than they'd been over Memorial Day, when he'd last seen them. Now they were settling in for a final blowout while remaining somehow poised for the end of indulgence, for the sobriety and discipline of returning to regular hours, meals, and habits. The heat and humidity of the city, its dirt, and the malaise of August had been rubbed off everyone but Alice, Peter, and the girls. They decided to go for a swim to wash off the feel of the car and the smell of the mustardy roast beef sandwiches and potato chips they'd eaten on the way up. With Maebelle barking excitedly from the edge of the pool as she dodged the great swaths of water the girls splashed at her, the swim refreshed them all.

The house felt worn. The jumbo jar of mayonnaise—fresh and pristine when purchased for the summer back in May—was nearly empty, the remains inside flecked with what appeared to be bread crumbs and unmistakable neon yellow smears of French's mustard. The winter residue of mice traps and rodent droppings neglected in far corners that had been there in the spring had been removed, the fragrant little pellets purposefully wiped with organic spray cleaner or licked equally clean by a dog. The house carried an end-of-summer grime: children's sticky hands had stained the outdoor cushions around the pool Smurf blue; a quantity of red wine spilled on the porch boards made it appear as if someone had bled out at the entrance; the kitchen cabinets were messy with half-eaten boxes of stale crackers and rumpled bags of chips left open to soak up the wet August air; the refrigerator harbored odd bits of desiccated cheese, useless after being passed over for months in favor of the superior offerings each weekend's wave of guests brought from their city shopping at Zabar's or Murray's.

The ambitious wines that opened the summer had given way to the new world: New Zealand rather than French sauvignon blanc, red blends from Chile rather than the Barolo that the Donnes favored, and California rosé over bottles from Provence. There was no wine pride in evidence, and Peter suspected their half case of Bandol would be mixed with the inferior stuff, going unnoticed. After a summer of floating ice cubes in wineglasses, it no longer mattered what anyone drank. Quantity was all that mattered. The publishing types, a class several of their guests belonged to, had been indulging in long weekends since July. They tried to quell their anxiety with more wine, but the truth was that their manuscripts, submissions, and galleys had piled up, all the paper and words unruly and in need of sorting. The lengthy pretense of vacation had left them all worn and careless of themselves. Relaxing, come August, was a chore. Labor Day weekend was the merciful last of it.

The day drinking that began at lunch bled into early cocktails. Each glass was just one more serving of alcohol it was impossible to refuse before the big drought that most of them would start on Tuesday. Peter and Alice promised themselves they'd go on the wagon after the weekend but didn't discuss it for fear of being held to what might turn out to be a fleeting desire to feel put together, virtuous, clean—a desire that would dissipate as the reality of the first day of fall and its darkening sameness came upon them.

The dinners, along with the wine, had grown careless. Nobody would have served burgers for dinner back in May— back then it was skirt steak and fresh peas and new potatoes. Sweet corn dirty with black pepper, hefty peaches so sticky with juice they had to be eaten over the sink, and a rainbow of lush, globular tomatoes proclaimed the apogee of summer. The last invited lazy cooking—or not cooking at all. For the past month Peter and Alice had gorged on slapdash tomato-mayonnaise sandwiches on levain, bowls of oily fusilli with tomato, garlic,

and basil made tough by long days and overgrowth in dry soil;
sliced mozzarella so fresh it was still warm stacked against rows
of cut tomatoes and more of that tough basil torn to pretty bits.

For Friday dinner, Alice and Peter helped cook a version of their standard summer pasta with blackened squash
and stubby pine nuts from the giant grocery store on Route
28. The puny Chinese nuggets were as bitter as the bolted
basil. But it was all summer food. Everyone was as tired of
tomatoes as they were of listening for the clink of ice and
hum of air conditioners.

On Sunday, Peter and Wendy sat with their morning coffee on
the big screened-in porch overlooking the pasture. The others
had gone for a hike. He was far too hungover for any exertion
beyond lifting his coffee cup to his lips, and she was not a hiker.
In fact, she never walked if she could avoid it. Nibbling a cold
crust of grainy toast, Peter considered getting up for more coffee but he was terribly comfortable, the warm sun coming in
at an angle to cut the cool air of the porch, its hint of autumn
just discernible. The sun's angled rays had just reached him.
He felt like a spoiled cat.

How's your practice, Peter? It sounds like you're very busy.
Not everyone is, you know. We're dinosaurs.

It's going well enough. I suppose I'm lucky. You?

Very busy. I do have a few patients I'm not looking forward
to seeing again on Tuesday. It's the curse of getting away. One
in particular has practically spoiled my vacation.

She or he?

She.

Calling you? Or are you simply struggling with the course of her treatment?

No. No, I don't allow calls over August break—do you? she asked, surprised.

I have. I do. The patient is troubled. I was concerned, so I gave her my number. It hasn't been a problem. In fact, I like feeling necessary to her.

Really? Sounds messy. Are you concerned?

About her?

No. About yourself.

You really take such a strict line?

I do. I thought you did as well. It's how we were trained— last I checked.

I know. But none of the rules are set fast. Every patient, every case, is different.

Tell me about her.

I've been seeing her for just almost a year. She's twenty-six, bipolar. I've got her on 15 mg Zyprexa. No substance abuse. Creative. Wealthy. Smart.

Sounds like the whole package. Lucky you. Is her mania under control? Suicidal?

That's part of the reason I gave her my number. I've never lost a patient, and I don't intend to start now. She seems to be responding well to the calls.

How often do you talk to her?

Once a day. Sometimes we skip a day, but not often.

We?

He looked embarrassed.

Now I'm really concerned. Is she attractive?

Very.

Peter.

I know, he said, pausing to consider his options. The hikers would be gone for at least another half hour. He was weary of his secret. Maybe he should try talking it through. Wendy was savvier than Dr. March.

I don't like it, Peter. I really don't. It's very dangerous—for her and for you. Do you want to talk about it? I'd love to help, if I can.

Things with Alice are difficult—

Come on, she interrupted. This isn't about Alice. Try again?

Fair enough. He laughed. But it's not easy. My feelings have gotten into a nasty tangle over this one. Honestly? I'm very attracted to her.

Please tell me nothing inappropriate has happened.

It hasn't. Not with her. Nothing like that.

What then?

Fantasies. I can't seem to get them under control. My erotic imagination has been hijacked by my libido—that makes no sense. Anyway. I'm desperate—thinking of going back into treatment myself.

Maybe you should, she said, taking a sip of coffee as she leaned back in her silky robe, her perceptive black eyes assessing him silently for a moment before she continued. Erotic countertransference can be useful in treatment—when properly managed. She certainly seems to have evoked a powerful response in you. Has she returned the favor?

She has. Dream content for the most part. Some physical seduction but limited to presentation. Listen, I've tolerated my sexual feelings but not acted on them in session.

The defensive negation of my feelings could be dangerous. I can't just shut down. She's fragile. I've been careful to avoid withholding. I'm afraid I'll overcorrect, appear cold and indifferent.

Fragile? How convenient for you. Honestly. Go ahead and reward yourself for not listening to your fear, for not shutting her and yourself out. Nobody needs an aloof shrink, especially a girl with a bad case of erotic transference—which you've not helped, I need not add. But do you honestly believe you've avoided seductive behavior of your own when you've just admitted that you're attracted to her, that your fantasy life has been *hijacked* by her? It doesn't pass the smell test, Peter. We all know our unconscious feelings aren't consistently regulated. Your signaling to her has to be accounted for. You have to take responsibility for leading her on.

I'm sure you're right, he said, looking at the ground. On top of my guilt over whatever she may be experiencing, my own behavior has me entirely disgusted with myself.

Your fantasy life, as we're so politely referring to it here, isn't really the problem, however sordid—it's your schoolboy self that's most troubled by it. Work on that on your own time. Just be careful in session. Put away your johnson, and definitely put it away at work. Better, more experienced psychiatrists than you have made the mistake of slipping past the boundary by whittling it down to nothing. The temptation is immense. Don't think for a minute you're immune—you're not.

Oh, I know. But what makes you say put your johnson—who calls it that anyway, Wendy?—away at work? I never said it made an appearance there—since you've chosen to be so crass about it.

Well has it?—Don't answer that. I'm not an idiot—and I'm not frigid. I've had naughty moments. But never mind that. What about Alice? I cut you off at the start. You need to address these impulses in relation to her—she's very much at play. Sorry to be blunt, but being around you two is hell. The flow of rage is as good as a natural heat source. This is more about Alice than you'd like. Agreed?

I wish I didn't.

Sort yourself out, Peter. You can't ice out Alice while continuing to treat the patient—all the while privately playing out your feelings for the girl. Why don't you fuck Alice while fantasizing she's the patient? That would be an improvement.

You are wicked, Wendy. Maybe I will.

Saturday's dinner had taken too long and Alice had gotten as drunk as Peter. Even the girls had had a glass too many of wine— it only made their cheeks glow without turning them sour and mean as it did the adults. However green everyone might be, the Sunday before Labor Day was the real holiday and they'd started with spicy gin Bloody Marys—hair of the dog and all that.

After the hike, Alice spent the afternoon by the pool with Maebelle resting in the shade beneath her chair while Peter napped upstairs. She had claimed one of the luxurious chaise longues, worse for wear after the summer but nonetheless plush and comfortable. She smeared sunscreen on her chest and face—no point in ruining her skin now that the summer was practically behind her. The value of a tan was one of diminishing returns as the summer wound down. By November she'd be shopping for peels to rid herself of the freckles and spots.

All the promise of summer books, hoarded for lost pool-
side or beach days, had been consumed or tossed aside in disgust after one bite, like rotten fruit. Alice was close to finishing
the last book of the summer, a slightly trashy novel in spite of
its subdued, tasteful cover; warped from the pool water on her
hands, the pages extended from the spine in soft waves rather
than in a straight, tight line. Alice had managed to fully dunk
one novel in the pool in Sagaponack when she capsized her
lilo while escaping a bee. Most of the books she'd read since
late May were battered. Sand had burrowed deep between the
pages of many of them, concealing itself close to the spine.
She imagined finding the polished little particles if she reread
them, the feel of grit from a long-forgotten beach between her
fingers and the surprise of tasting salt on her tongue with no
sea in sight.

Deeply relieved the summer was over, Alice was ready
to have Peter out of the house and back to work in earnest.
She had an October 1 grant deadline to meet and she was
surprisingly weary of travel. Bette and Emile would be leaving
Monday afternoon out of Newburgh's Stewart Airport—they'd
drop them on the way home. That was easy, but the thought
of losing them again after such a brief reunion flattened the
promise of autumn's cooler air, sweaters, jeans, and boots. She
was ready for a change of wardrobe—for the flimsy clothes of
the hot months to give way to sturdier, more substantial fabric,
something to hold her together the way a cozy sweater could.
As Alice was musing about the feel of pulling on her favorite
jeans after three months without wearing them, she looked up
to see Wendy wandering down the neatly clipped grass on the
boarder of the dahlia bed, her bustiness barely covered by her

red bikini top, a gauzy cover-up concealing her legs and hips, a tall, cool pinky-orange drink in each hand.

Have you a cigarette, Alice? She whispered, handing her the Aperol spritz.

Since when do you smoke? And who says I do?

Oh, it takes one to know one. I don't really smoke much anymore. I just like to bum one now and again. And I've had just enough to drink—never mind the hour—that I've got a case of the fuck-its.

Retrieving two cigarettes from the pack in her straw beach bag, Alice took them between her lips and lit them simultaneously, handing one to Wendy after the first pull.

Aren't you the professional, Wendy laughed, taking the lit cigarette and inhaling deeply. The smoke coming out of her nose gave her a villainous affect as it billowed up to the sky, twisting and eddying like cream in hot coffee.

I am so ready to go back to work. You must be excited to finish your grant.

Yes, the NSF funds very quickly—there's a chance I could begin by January. It's scary—good scary. I'm sure Peter is pleased. He's a bit sick of me.

I doubt that. He adores you.

You think?

I do.

Maybe.

You two okay?

Yeah, we'll be fine. What else is there? Losing Maebelle was devastating. He was probably half relieved she disappeared. She forced a laugh. Have you ever heard of a man jealous of a dog?

How so?

He resents the way I show my affection to her.

Do you hear yourself? She smiled.

What?

You should take it as a compliment. I would. Or, if you can't, at least read it. He's hungry, Alice. I know you're pretty self-sufficient, but he's not. I'm not even talking about sex. I'm talking about touch. He's lonely.

We're all lonely.

Are we? I'm not. I'm so tired of William I could move to a hotel. I listen to my patients talk all day, and then I come home to his chatter. It's sweet, but I never have a moment alone. It's not the physical I mind—I still love sex—surely you do, too.

Maybe. I've realized I'm not what is often called a generous lover. I'm stingy—maybe in bed as much as anywhere else. I get pleasure but not pleasure giving pleasure—and that's the crux of it, isn't it? Besides, it's been so long. That level of intimacy with Peter feels dangerous. God, that's such a strange thing to say about him. He's by far the most important person in my life—besides the girls—and yet I have so much trouble being open with him. Maybe we both withhold ourselves. Stand back in safety. Our relationship has been more like a complicated friendship than a marriage. And now sex has become an alien concept.

What about between you and someone else? Alice thought there was a suggestion hidden in there somewhere.

Well, Alice laughed. Maybe I can imagine sex with someone else. I just know too much, and besides, haven't you heard? Nobody has sex anymore.

I think you may be right. More and more of my patients are declaring they're done with it—too many great sex toys and too much porn. I don't think it bodes well for human civilization—do you?

I'm not sure I care. It's all melting anyway. Maybe it'll lead to fewer babies. Peter has his work; I have mine. We're mutually supportive when it comes to the girls, the apartment, his parents. If something happens to me—good or bad—Peter's still the first one I want to tell. It's as if my reality requires his reaction, and he always gives it to me. Lately, though, he seems more remote than usual—and angrier. You should see the state a crowded subway platform puts him in.

Tell me more, said Wendy. She'd slipped into shrink mode. Alice didn't mind—so long as she didn't have to hear about *validation* or *telling X to Peter*. Couple's therapy was such an abomination.

I don't exactly understand his work—your work, Alice said, distracted by Wendy's shift in tone. It all seems so vague and self-indulgent. Sorry. I don't mean you. I mean the patients.

Peter is self-indulgent. He's a child. Men are babies—king babies.

Was that really what I just said?

Pretty much. I'd say it was more palatable to call his patients self-indulgent.

So why should I care—about how he runs his practice or whether his patients need his treatment?

Maybe you care more than you think? Maybe you're a little jealous of his patients? It's not unusual. William is constantly complaining I expend my warmth at work and forget to save any for him. He loves it when I'm not working. It's true. We get closer when my mind isn't wrapped up in my patients' concerns. It's a work hazard.

I guess I know that. It's just that something feels different lately.

Has Peter been more present since he started—

Alice paused, waiting for her to finish and then filled in for her. Vacation? No, if anything he's even more remote. And he's taking a patient's calls at home. Did he tell you that?

He did.

Do you approve?

It's really not for me to approve or not, Wendy said before adding, I suggested to him that I thought it wasn't the best practice—for him or the patient.

But he knows that. So why is he doing it now, after twenty years? I do wonder—but then, part of me doesn't want to know.

Perhaps he's frustrated you withhold your affection, and you're jealous of his patients. It would seem you two could discuss this.

Not likely.

Really?

No. We don't talk about *us*. Alice paused. To hell with it, she thought, Just say it. I had an affair.

Good for you, said Wendy flatly.

Seriously? Aren't you horrified?

Of course not. I'm used to it. Is it over?

Actually, yes. It was a one-off.

Good. That's nice and clean. Tell me more, she said with a smile, as if anticipating the juicy details.

At the time—in the moment—it was fantastic. I realized I do want sex—I miss sex. I was so attracted to him. He's a gorgeous man and smart, too. As she said the words the memory of her last humiliating conversation with George returned, and at that the playfulness drained from her body, the awful memory of their exchange stripping her energy.

Peter's not too bad himself.

I can't even see Peter anymore, Alice said. Besides, he's as bored with me as I am with him. Wendy, it was exciting to seduce and be seduced. The experience of skin on skin, even afterward, when we fell asleep together reminded me of early days with Peter. The smell of a man in the bed. I love that smell—most of the time.

Peter doesn't know?

Not a chance. Why tell him? There's nothing to gain.

I would argue there is, she said seriously. The truth isn't so disposable as all that. It carries an intrinsic value—in life and especially in relationships. Deception necessarily creates distance. It takes a lot of energy to protect a secret. You can't be fully present—either of you—when you're holding on to shame. And unless you're a sociopath, you're going to be carrying around some shame with every secret you hold on to.

I'm not at all sure he deserves to know. Besides, I like my secret.

That's because it protects you. It holds you apart where you're most comfortable. I know you've long kept a zone of privacy, and I respect it—within limits. Infidelity—whether it's a lack of fealty to the other purely in mind or physical betrayal—can be good for a marriage if it's taken as an opportunity to reassess. What are you two missing in one another? In telling him, you'd be forced into a vulnerable position—and so would he because he'd be humiliated. Just watch his rage—and, for that matter, your own. If you can both survive the conversation you might be surprised at the results. You're out of sync. That you've strayed for the first time in twenty-one, twenty years? It's not a mistake—it's an opportunity. And whatever is going on with Peter and his patient can be brought into the conversation.

Alice looked at the sky. White cumulus clouds were building on the horizon, their massive billowing centers boiling with energy. She knew Wendy was right. Still, she half regretted telling her. She'd put George behind her after their not-lunch at Union Square Cafe. Now he was out again—here in the open air, mixing with the smell of chlorine, sunscreen, and cut grass. The indiscretion, as she'd taken to calling it in her mind, felt long ago. Wendy seemed to be suggesting she should pay attention to Peter's patient, that it somehow mattered. There was an assumption of illicit behavior in the phone calls that Alice had tried to shrug off. She half wondered what Wendy really knew.

Wendy's voice in the world of classical physics was a wave that carried various frequencies to Alice's ears that in turn received the sound and decoded it into meaning through language. But the swirling currents of subatomic particles, the excitable neuronal cells, around and in her surely played a part just as they did in a murmuration. How else to explain the brain's ability to turn sound into meaning and meaning into the sickening emotion Alice felt descending on her at Wendy's nuanced emphasis on Peter's demanding patient? The relationship between energy and information was undeniable—Alice could feel the energy of this information coursing through her body. Or maybe it was the Aperol? Trying to think of something else, she considered the billions of cells that formed her, just one more expression of collective intel-ligence. A single starling disengaged from any level of higher organization was as pathetic and useless as a single neuron cut off from the complete brain or an ant lifted away from the scent trails and purposeful movement of its group—reduced to nothing in the absence of its hive mind.

This Lisbeth—for surely that's who it was, that first call of vacation, pre-fight—was an inconsequential ball of energy. She was probably pretty and smart and young, but what did that matter? What if Peter were fucking her? Or having phone sex? She didn't know what was best for Peter—didn't even want to know. It was almost a relief to think he'd given up on her. Whatever mess he was in over his patient, it was his mess. It meant nothing to her so long as he contained it.

Alice wanted their life together. All the energy she'd expended on George, from her fantasies to misreading him, taught her how exhausting it was to be with someone new. If she left Peter, she might find someone new, even fall in love afresh, and then before she could stop herself she'd lose track of her own desire as she worked to please, flatter, and know him. How wasteful and tiresome. She was as autonomous with Peter as he was with her—their knowledge and history cemented a terrifying and deeply reassuring continuity. Sure, she would like him to find her more interesting, but she had friends and colleagues to fill that role. The idea that there was something or someone better out there was a lie, one that would in the end keep her from herself at a moment when she was just relocating who she'd once been, before the girls and, strangely, even before Peter.

* * *

Between trying to find everyone, helping to clean, and trying not to forget anything, the goodbyes took too long. All four of them were finally in the car with Peter negotiating the windy road before pulling onto I-90 West. Soon, he was blowing by cars at 85 mph. Why did he drive so fast? They had plenty of time before the flight.

The girls sat in the back, earbuds in. How glorious—how perfect they were. Alice didn't want to be nineteen again—it had been confusing, and she'd been so lonely. Strangely, Bette and Emile didn't seem unhappy. Why and how were they so well adjusted? Was it their internet education, her mothering, Peter's warmth and affection for them, or something at once more simple and complex—their brains and bodies working smoothly as systems in an environment that supported them?

These systems, the same ones that made up all of their bodies, were in states of continual flow marked by self-entangled stream lines, whorls, spiral vortices. The chaos on every level of life was a patterned order determined by some force that kept entropy from winning—or at least from winning too fast. This force, this strange attractor that kept it all in symmetrical order was, as people liked to say, *psychoanalytically suggestive*. Indeed, thought Alice.

The harmony within Bette's and Emile's systems was smoother than that within hers or Peter's. As they aged, the generative forces that had formed them also fomented drag and disorder throughout their bodies. The law of entropy was degrading them, the symmetry of patterns on every level marred by mistakes. Eventually, in death, it would cease to cohere as a whole. The necessary orderly work of each proton, neuron, atom, and cell was dissipating the way at dusk starlings return to the earth, falling out of their murmuration bird by bird to rest alone in the absence of daylight. Without the energy that drove order there was a dismal void.

The repeating patterns in nature were truly stunning, she thought, as she stared back at her daughters' shiny hair, dimpled skin, smooth forms, and most sensational of all—a thing she could not see but felt—their intelligence, humanity and, dare she think it, their spirits. Each one had an essence that exceeded any reductive impulse. Nobody had yet come close to grasping how a human, as a complex system, could in sum contain the capacity for so surprising and inexplicable a thing as a sense of humor, memory, empathy, lust, fear, or sadness. These qualities, really these intelligences, existed both nowhere and everywhere at once. Without each other to discern the differences, to know the details as well as they know each other, they didn't exist—not fully, in all their vain, glorious complexity.

As they entered the grounds of the airport, Alice saw that Bette and Emile had fallen asleep with their headphones on. The sight of them leaning against each other, their faces slack, reminded Alice of all the sleeps she'd woken them from and how each one had passed her by—particular and worth preserving only now, as the familiar act threatened to be taken from her. Alice reached back between the seats, gently rubbing one of her daughter's legs and then the other daughter's to rouse them. They'd always been easy to wake, coming to with a friendly smile.

We're here?

Wow. I slept.

Here, Alice replied. Got everything? Don't forget your charger, she said, pulling the cord from the outlet in front and handing it back. The first thing each of them did as they came to was look at their phones for whatever excitement the hive had offered up to them. Always generative, leaderless, changing, and yet orderly. Had humans somehow tipped the balance of communication into an unstoppable realm with the use of social media? What caused the tip into criticality just before information went viral? After a certain point, there was no host. The information itself surpassed the human that initiated it; the information gained a kind of symbiotic intelligence as it accumulated energy through the replication of human engagement as they liked, commented, posted, and reposted.

As they pulled their massive suitcases onto the curb, a state trooper waved at Peter to move on. A robotic recorded voice droned: *No parking. Unloading and loading only.* Peter stared at the three women, astonished at the impossible riches before him. To belong to them seemed an implausible good. He hugged his two girls, a lingering embrace that was his effort to communicate love in raw form, enough of it to last them until Thanksgiving, when he would see them next, when he would again fill them up as best he could with the physical expression of all he felt. Alice said goodbye, her throat tight, eyes wet. She wanted to linger, to take them to their gate and wait with them so she could stand in the massive window inside the terminal and wave at their faces in the plane's little oval windows until the giant bird disappeared from her sight. But such goodbyes were long past, preserved on film as an ideal and in the most distant recesses of her own memory. The policeman whistled, the shrill sound defining impatience.

Back in the car, Alice and Peter drove in silence, nothing reaching them but the sound of the grooved road whir-
ring beneath the tires. She couldn't be what he wanted any
more than he could be what she wanted. But maybe it was
enough—however many gaps and crevasses might bar the
distance between them.

The interior of the car dimmed as the sun fell long past
its midpoint on its descent down the deep blue sky. It was the
color of the most desirable jewel. Peter signaled and maneuvered in front of a car moving too slowly in the right lane.
Accelerating past the pokey impediment, the car lurched up
a gear as he took the exit for New York City, I-87 South, much
too fast, the centrifugal force pressing Alice against the door
as the wide curve brought them round. Bracing herself against
the dashboard, she looked at him, raising both eyebrows with
a bemused look as if to say, *What the hell?* He turned to meet
her eye, giving her a knowing, conspiratorial glance.

Ready? he said, as if they were about to launch into orbit.

Always, Alice replied, although she wasn't sure for what.

Acknowledgements

This novel was elicited by my agent and mentor, Sarah Chalfant of the Wylie Agency. It wouldn't exist without her. I will always be grateful to her for believing that I could—and should—write this story. I owe an immense debt to the talented, dedicated Elisabeth Schmitz, my editor and friend at Grove Atlantic. Thanks to Katie Raissian for her outstanding editing, to Julia Berner-Tobin for her endless work on the manuscript, and to Gretchen Mergenthaler for the gorgeous cover art. To all the friends who so graciously hosted me over the course of various summers—you know who you are—I hope this book won't cause you to strike me from the guest list. To my children, Penn and Harriet Garner LeFavour, I can only say you're everything good. Finally, thanks go to my husband Dwight Garner for the humor, support, and love that make my days joyful.